Built for Power

Women of Power Series

Kathleen Brooks

Cover art by Calista Taylor
http://www.coversbycali.com

Acknowledgments

I have been blessed with some wonderful friends over the years and these three ladies are no exception. They helped answer all my questions. I even got my own pink Bullard hard hat! Thank you, Wells, Rebekah, and Kate, for the frantic texts and weird "what-if's" I posed to y'all.

I also have to send a big shout-out to Alicia, Amanda, and Lucy from my Krew for helping me with all things British. And to my whole Krew for all the support and fun we have. Thank you, ladies!

Prologue

"There's a *girl* in our class," Nick said as if her sex were a curse. "She'll probably break a nail and start crying."

Bree Simpson's archenemy sauntered into shop class and grabbed his safety goggles. He made sure to stop at every table along the way to his station to whisper a joke at Bree's expense. Bree smiled as if his barbs didn't hurt and gathered the equipment needed to build a birdhouse.

"What do you think, boys? I give her one class."

"One class to what?" Bree asked with mock confusion. "To fall helplessly in love with you? To swoon at your feet over your manly use of a saw? Or maybe to realize how full of shi . . ."

"Miss Simpson!"

Bree batted her eyes at her teacher. "Yes, Mr. Voss?" she asked innocently.

"Enough talking. It's time to build."

"You think you run with the big dogs, do you?" Nick hissed.

"No. Why would I want to do that? I'll be the one with the dog whistle telling you where to run and when to sit and beg." Bree slid her goggles into place. Nick's rant became lost in the buzz of the table saw.

Bree measured the wood and, with a steady hand, drew the cut lines with her pencil. She moved the metal ruler and measured again before cutting. The high pitch of the saw increased as she slowly but steadily pushed the wood through. Dust hit her goggles and lodged in her strawberry blonde hair, currently thrown up in a messy bun. The smell of freshly cut wood hung in the air. Bree smiled as she made cut after cut.

"Look at that mess of wood she has over there, boys. I told you she couldn't do it. All I have to do is cut the roof and I am *d-o-n-e*," Nick yelled to his friends over the hammering.

Bree smiled again as she looked at her large pile of cut pieces and then at Nick's respectable, but simple, birdhouse. She picked up her hammer and with two good whacks, just like her father taught her, drove the nail home.

After remeasuring every piece, she assembled her birdhouse. No piece of wood was longer than the others. Every piece fit perfectly. After drilling a few quick holes, she hammered a peg in front of each door and smiled. Her birdhouse was done. She glanced up. No one was paying attention to her. Nick was busy recutting the roof of his house. It gave her time to admire her creation. She felt alive when she built things. It was a rush—the precise measuring, configuring the pieces of the puzzle—bringing the vision to life.

Bree had taken this class as a way to see if the fun she had building things with her dad was more than a hobby. And it was. She felt the excitement of engineering a birdhouse, even if it was just for shop class, run through her body. Her father had encouraged her to take the class and now she was glad she did—even if she had to put up with the boys teasing her. But her dad had also taught her how to handle them.

"Bree, just smile and let it wash over you. Everyone has to learn how to deal with bullies. You'll have them when you're six years old, when you're sixteen, and when you're sixty. Sometimes keeping to the high road is enough. But sometimes you need to make your voice heard without saying a word."

As Bree walked to the front of the class, she did just that. She sat her five-bedroom birdhouse next to Nick's slightly crooked one without saying a single word. Her house was a bird mansion. There were three "rooms" on the bottom with two on the second story. An elegantly sloped roof finished the house beautifully.

Bree picked up her backpack and walked out the door to the sounds of the other boys teasing Nick.

Chapter One

Bree Simpson kicked off her designer heels and shoved her feet into steel-toed boots. She placed the pink hard hat over her perfectly coiffed hair and picked up the hem of her long, gold gown. Not watching where she stepped, she marched over the mud and gravel to the trailer housing the offices for the corporate center build.

"Marcus, what's going on?" Bree asked as she flung open the door.

Her senior site manager, Marcus Phillips, looked up from his desk with a slight grimace. The trailer was lit only by the low glow of a single lamp. Despite the darkness, Bree could still make out the green piece of paper.

"This was tacked to the door. The security guard found it. It has your name on it."

"You called me down here for this? I'm in the middle of a black tie event." Bree tried to control her hands as she snatched the envelope from his. "What are you doing here this late anyway?"

"Sorry to interrupt the event. I've seen you get these notes before and thought this might be important. Like maybe you forgot to pick it up. I didn't mean for you to leave the banquet. I thought you could pick it up when you were on your way home."

Bree let out a breath. She wasn't mad. Well, not mad at Marcus anyway. "It's okay. It was just a bunch of men toasting how great they are. They probably won't even notice I'm gone. I can sneak back in and no one will be the wiser."

"You were robbed. You should have been Builder of the Year," Marcus protested for the hundredth time.

"You have to be nominated first, and they'll never nominate me. Why don't you grab a suit coat and join me. There's a bunch of beautiful twenty-something daughters running around," Bree coaxed. Marcus was only twenty-nine. He had advanced to a high-level position because he lived and breathed work. So, despite her total lack of love life, Bree was determined to help him find someone special.

"As if I'd date someone whose father wouldn't recognize the good work you do simply because you're a woman," Marcus scoffed.

"Don't hate the player; hate the game." Bree teased. After all these years, she was still in shop class . . . just on a much larger scale. "Well, if you want to join me, you know where I'll be."

"Don't hold your breath. I'm trying to anticipate the architect's changes and get the materials ordered so we don't fall further behind." Marcus ran his hand over his buzzed blond hair. His blue eyes were tired and Bree felt the maternal need to take care of her young site manager despite being just a couple years older.

"You still haven't received the changes?" Bree asked in astonishment. After the tongue-lashing she'd delivered to Mr. Ward's secretary, she was sure he would get the final plans to Marcus quickly.

"Nope. I called and was told Mr. Ward was out of the office. After leaving four voicemails, sending eight emails, and trying to bribe his secretary, I finally gave up and decided to order what I think needs to be ordered."

No wonder he looked tried and stressed. "Go home and relax. Or better, go on a date or two," Bree called as she clutched the green envelope and headed for the door.

"What about Mr. Ward?"

"Oh, I'll take care of Mr. Ward. Don't you worry."

Bree stomped her way to the car and pulled out her small clutch. She ripped it open, then pulled out her lipstick and her cell phone — the only two things that would fit in it. "Troy, I'm sorry to wake you, but I need to get to London."

She heard Simpson Global's pilot sit up in bed and run his hand over his face in an attempt to wake up. "Yes, ma'am."

Bree winced. She hated being called ma'am. "How long?"

"Wheels up in an hour."

"Aye, aye, captain!"

"Why do I work for you again?"

"You get to fly a really cool plane and secretly you love us," Bree teased the retired Air Force pilot.

A grunt was all Bree heard before the line went dead. Gracefully sliding into her seat, she picked up the green envelope from where she had flung it. She hated the way her hands trembled as she tore it open. She'd been receiving these notes ever since she started the corporate center build. At first they'd been taunts. But then they had turned dark and ugly.

Bree took a breath and pulled out the folded paper. She slowly unfolded it and stared at the now familiar type.

You looked lovely tonight at the banquet. If you want to wear fancy dresses anytime again, you need to heed my warnings. Your time is running out. Step down from the corporate center project and go back to your manicures, teas, and fancy dresses.

Bree felt her mouth go dry. The notes had started as threats against the corporate center build. At first she thought they might be from eco-terrorists trying to stop the project. But then the notes had turned personal. They had commented on what she was wearing and how she shouldn't be tempting the men she worked with. So she had begun to think they were just sexist. However, right after the foundation was laid, the threats had turned violent, telling her to step down and hire someone else to head the project or she'd be sorry.

Things had started happening at the work site. Tools had been stolen or destroyed. Cars had been keyed. Nasty things had been spray-painted on the perimeter walls about her. And then the notes had started threatening her life if she didn't step down and clean house. It was clear someone was not happy that she had bought into this project. She had broken with local customs by hiring the workers she wanted, and not the "buddies" who thought they were owed every job. The trouble was, there were too many of them to count. It was why she went to the dinner tonight. She was hoping to get some clue as to who was sending her these notes. Unfortunately, all she got was par for the course and a rubber chicken dinner.

Some of the men approved of the changes she was bringing to the industry while others made her the butt of their jokes. It had only helped her cut her suspects from fifty to twenty-five. She had left frustrated at the fact she didn't know how to trim the list of suspects down anymore.

Bree didn't take these threats seriously, but she'd be

stupid not to look into them. Of the twenty-five or so people who didn't approve of her, ten were incredibly outspoken about it, and they'd all been at the party. However, four of them had left the party early enough to leave the note for her at the construction site. Finally, a clue!

Bree opened the list of names on her cell phone and began to cross them off until only the four remained. Carey Robins, Trevor Marion, Jeff Henderson, and Louis Garcia. She'd look into each of them when she got back. Eventually one of them would do something to give himself away.

In the meantime, she admitted that she couldn't control what this bully did or tried to do, but she could control her project. If her time was coming to an end, the least she could do was get her architect's *arse* on task.

Bree stomped one steel-toe-clad foot in front of Mr. Ward's secretary. She hadn't bothered to go home and when she boarded the family jet to London, she discovered there was no change of clothes in the closet. She imagined she'd looked somewhat like a serial killer prom queen as she stood with big boots and a shiny gold evening gown with a tight bodice that hugged her curves and pooled around her feet. Her perfectly coiffed hair had started to slip, and she felt like breaking down the closed door to Mr. Ward's office with an axe.

"What do you mean, Mr. Ward won't see me?" Bree asked with all the restraint she had. "It's easy. Pick up the phone and tell him I'm here from Atlanta and demand to see him."

The snooty secretary, whom she and her assistant, Noah, had been calling Mrs. Snobgrass, looked down her pointy nose at her and in her perfect British accent said, "It's rather impossible for you to see someone who is not here."

Bree rolled her eyes. "You know, you could have just said that in the first place. Fine. I will sit and wait until he gets back."

"That will be a rather long wait whilst Mr. Ward travels. He's visiting his sites and could be gone this entire week. Tea?"

Fire raced up Bree's face and she was pretty sure steam was coming from her ears. "I just flew halfway across the world to see him. The hundred times I, or my assistant, called this week, you could have told us that and saved me this trip! Where is he right now?"

If possible, Mr. Ward's secretary looked farther down her nose as she reluctantly thumbed through her desk calendar. "Dubai. I'll tell him you came to call. Where are you staying and I'll notify you when he arrives."

"I'm not staying. I run a major corporation, and I don't have time to just sit here and wait for him to decide my hundred-million-dollar project is worth his time. What you need to do is pick up the phone, call his cell, and tell him he'd better *bloody* well get back here before I fire him."

Bree struggled to restrain her temper but Mrs. Snobgrass didn't seem to have any trouble controlling hers. "I will be sure to give him your message. Does he have your number?"

Bree slammed her card down on the table and stormed from the room with her gold train flowing behind her.

Logan Ward was exhausted. It was the middle of the night

when his plane from Dubai landed at Heathrow International Airport in London. He'd been out of the office for over two weeks visiting the European and Middle East builds his architectural firm were designing. He'd finalized plans, he'd changed plans on-site, and he'd said, "Sure, we can do that," to far too many crazy things to even remember.

Today he was going to work from home and sleep. He hailed a cab and headed to the office. He was sure Beatrice had a stack of work for him on his desk. She'd sent the emergencies to him, but the rest he'd have to try to get done tomorrow.

Logan took a deep breath and looked out the window for the long drive down the M4 into London. The cab turned toward the River Thames. Logan watched as they drove past Big Ben and neared his office. He'd been all over the world, and as he got out of the cab, he realized how much he missed home. It seemed the office had been his home for the past ten years. As he paid the cab driver, he looked up at the old stone building with large rectangular windows. He should be partner by now.

The old guard would never allow it, though. He was an outsider and they were too eager to collect their fat cuts of the profits that Logan brought to the firm. Not that he wasn't paid well, he was. But he was almost thirty-five years old and a "good job, old chap" with a pat on the back wasn't cutting it for him anymore.

Unlocking the door to his office, he almost groaned out loud when he saw the huge stack of messages waiting on his large desk. Logan dropped his bags and fell into his chair, admitting the likelihood of getting home was looking slimmer and slimmer. He picked up the messages and thumbed through them. B. Simpson, B. Simpson, B.

Simpson, Noah from Simpson Steel and Construction, and then the doozy: *B. Simpson stopped by office. Threatened to fire you.*

Logan laid the back of his head against his chair and stared up at the ceiling. He should have never taken this job . . . as if it were a choice. One of the owners of this corporate center in Atlanta, Georgia, was a friend of the founder of his architectural firm. It was probably this Mr. Simpson. Logan could see him wanting gold flying buttresses now. He had been going through Logan's boss for all the changes to the design, but he guessed being friends only went so far in dealing with his crazy whims. Logan pulled out the file and shook his head. He'd changed the plans no fewer than ten times. Logan was sure the construction manager was losing his mind, because God knows *he* was.

But this was it. He didn't want another damn message from Mr. Simpson and he sure as hell wasn't making any more changes to the perfect design he'd turned in already. Well, he guessed it was a good thing he didn't unpack. It looked like he was heading to Atlanta to give B. Simpson a piece of his mind.

Chapter Two

Bree zipped the royal blue sundress outlined with white ribbon and slid her feet into a pair of wedges. After arriving home from England, she'd told Marcus to order whatever was needed for the latest plans he'd received. When she got hold of Mr. Ward, she was going to tell him they couldn't afford to wait on his uncertainty. She'd heard many wonderful things about him, but he was being so indecisive she couldn't imagine why everyone loved him so much.

Bree blew out a breath as she tried to push Mr. Ward from her mind. Today was her older sister Elle and Drake's wedding shower, and she had to prepare for it. Bree and her younger sister, Allegra, knew the pitfalls of a wedding shower after being ambushed at the last one. Bree looked in the mirror and tried to find a serene smile. "Why, no, I'm not dating anyone. Yes, I know I'm not getting any younger. No, I don't feel unfulfilled with my life because I'm not married," she practiced saying to her reflection.

Elle and Drake defied the odds. They were two immensely powerful people who found a way to make the quality of their time together more important than the quantity of it. She'd never seen her sister happier and Drake already felt like another brother. Speaking of brothers . . .

"Hello, Reid," Bree said into her phone. Reid, the oldest

of the Simpson clan, was probably trying to find any excuse to skip the couple's shower this afternoon.

"Yeah, so I don't think I can make it today," Reid started.

"Washing your hair?" Bree asked sweetly.

"If it gets me out of going to this thing, then yeah."

Bree let out a long-suffering sigh that only sisters with brothers could make. "Reid, if Allegra and I have to be subjected to this, then so do you. You're Elle's one and only brother. You have to be there. Besides, Mallory just told Elle she can't make it, and Elle's devastated that her best friend can't come. You can't do this to her. So grow a pair and get your butt over there to support your sister."

"Well, I guess I can make an appearance. I've heard showers are a good place to pick up women."

"I think you were adopted," Bree said dryly before hanging up to the sounds of Reid's chuckles.

Bree grabbed the present and her keys and headed out the front door. When she saw her car, she knew something was wrong but couldn't tell what it was until she looked down. The tires were flat. She felt her chest tighten as she looked wildly around. Was the person who did this still here or was it a freak accident? As she stepped closer to the car, she got her answer. The tires were slashed.

Stepping around the car, Bree felt all the blood drain to her feet as her body went numb with shock. In bright pink spray paint were the words *I like getting nailed by big hammers*. She stared at the letters as cars drove by and honked their approval. Her face went red with embarrassment, but it quickly turned to anger. Bree dug around her purse and pulled out her cell phone. She called the police and then a tow truck.

There was really only one person she could call who was going to the shower and who had bad enough eyesight that she might not notice the neon pink spray paint. While she waited, she sent a text to Mallory to ask her to dig up some dirt on Logan Ward. She wasn't above blackmail to get this job done.

Standing on the side of the road as far away from her car as possible while the tow truck hooked it up, Bree held out her hand and waved. The red sporty convertible swerved across the road and came to a screeching halt.

"Hello, dear."

"Hi, Shirley. Thanks for picking me up." Bree smiled at her father's former secretary who was now the office manager for Simpson Global. Shirley wouldn't tell anyone her real age, but Bree and her sisters were pretty sure it was well past eighty.

"No problem. Just don't plan on a ride home. I'm picking up a nice young buck. These parties are easy pickings. So are fraternity parties for that matter."

Bree was pretty sure she'd just found Reid's birth parent. Margaret, their mother, would never dream of picking up men half her age . . . or younger. No, Margaret was a stickler for Southern manners. It didn't matter that she was born poor. She believed manners made the woman. However, it also didn't stop her and Shirley from being close friends. In fact, Shirley acted as if Margaret were her daughter and Bree and the rest of the Simpson gang were her grandkids. Which worked out perfectly for Bree, because who else could she have called with a sexual innuendo written on her car?

"That's fine. I'm sure Allegra can take me home. Happy hunting," Bree said as she tried to angle her body to shield her car as they drove by. Too bad it didn't work.

"Hammer, huh? Men. Always overvaluing what's between their legs. I'd say it's more like a pickle, maybe a zucchini if you're lucky," Shirley said casually as she sped off down the street. Bree groaned, waiting for the inquisition, but it never came.

"I'm telling you, I've got some tricks up my sleeve. You don't live as many years as I do without learning a thing or two. There was this one time during the war I walked into a bar where all these sailors were on day pass and let me tell you . . ." Bree stuck her fingers in her ears and started humming. Maybe she should have called Allegra after all.

Bree got out of the sports car and walked around to the tiny trunk to help Shirley pull out her walker. *Blink if you think I'm sexy* was hanging between the handles of the walker. Bree shook her head as Shirley gave her a wink and headed for the house.

Leaning into the back seat, Bree picked up the gifts for Elle and Drake, followed Shirley inside, and almost laughed out loud when she saw her mother's living room set up like a middle school dance. The girls were all in a circle on one side of the room talking while the men stood along the other side looking horribly uncomfortable.

Reid came out of the kitchen with a handful of beers. As he passed Bree, he leaned over and kissed her cheek. "Hey, sis. Please tell mom men don't drink those fruity drinks. If we're going to suffer through this, sneak us the good stuff, will ya?"

"Seriously? It's only two hours long."

"Games, Bree. There are shower games," Reid said almost desperately.

Bree cringed. "In that case, I may join you."

Reid darted away as Aunt Flory zeroed in on Bree.

"Coward!" Bree hissed at her brother's retreating back. "Hi, Aunt Flory."

"Oh, you poor dear! It must be so hard for you to be here." Aunt Flory's dyed red hair bobbed as she pooh-poohed Bree.

"Um, no. I'm actually pretty happy to be here." Bree put on her best smile and searched the room for a rescue. Allegra was hiding behind a ficus tree and Reid was doing his best to use Finn, Elle's former driver who had been promoted to sports agent when he earned his law degree, as a shield.

"To see your sister so happy and your cousin, my baby, so in love with Phillip, must hurt right here." Flory thumped her chest over her heart.

"Ah, but they're stuck with one hammer now. I like all kinds of hammers." Bree smiled before doing the fake wave to an imaginary person across the room and leaving her aunt standing in total confusion.

She knew she only had minutes until her mother found her and called her to task for saying something crude, but Aunt Flory had always looked out for number one and never really cared about them until they became rich. Now they just tolerated her for the sake of Cousin Mary. Mary had blossomed when she stepped away from her negative mother and found love with Drake's best friend and assistant, Phillip. He was outgoing, funny, and somehow had broken through Mary's shell and brought her true self out.

"Hammers? Really, Bree?" Her mother had caught her before she'd made it to the hiding spot behind the ficus tree.

Bree looked at her mother decked out in her white trousers and bright yellow silk shirt and sighed. Reid had been right to try to get out of coming, but she loved Elle and would somehow find the inner peace to survive this.

"You're thirty-one years old and you're talking about *hammers*? If only *hammers* were the truth, then at least there'd be a shot of getting married! Now mind your *P*s and *Q*s and mingle. And for God's sake, get your sister out from behind that tree and don't you dare sneak a bottle of bourbon for your brother. Alma! It's so good to see you again." Bree's mother disappeared just as fast as she had appeared.

"We've been busted," Bree told Allegra.

"Shhh. I don't want Aunt Flory to find me. Mom's friends have asked me constantly about my love life." Allegra, the VP of Simpson Fashion, must have planned her hiding spot. The beautiful jungle-green sheath dress she wore blended perfectly with the ficus.

"Yeah, she already caught me. Where did Mom hide the bourbon? It's going to be a long evening and this fruity concoction isn't gonna cut it."

"Behind her cookbooks. Oh, crap." Allegra looked up and saw Aunt Flory lock eyes with her. "I think I've been found. Thanks a lot, sis."

"Love ya!" Bree giggled as she hurried away to talk to Elle.

Bree fought her way through the crowd of women toward her older sister. "Elle," Bree called out. Elle smiled at her and held out her hand, parting the crowd so she was able to hug her sister.

"Excuse me, ladies. I have to talk maid of honor stuff with my sister," Elle said in her politest boardroom voice. The reaction was immediate as they all smiled and, with hungry eyes, turned on the men. "Oh dear, Aunt Flory has Allegra cornered."

"This is what I call a moral dilemma. Save her but sacrifice myself or save myself," Bree said seriously.

"You may not have to. Look," Elle gave a quick glance to where Finn was extricating himself from the clutches of the women. And who could blame them. Finn was a retired major league baseball player and six foot three inches of muscled hotness. The light tan suit contrasted with his dark skin, giving him an appealing look of casual elegance. Too bad she thought of him more as a little brother, even if they were the same age.

"What's going on there?" Bree wondered as she and Elle watched Finn walk over to Allegra and wrap his arm around her.

"I don't know, but I really want to find out. Look how wide Aunt Flory's eyes are. I wonder what he said."

"You don't think they're together, do you? I mean, look at how he's looking at her. I'm growing hot all the way over here," Bree teased.

"No kidding. But as far as I know, Allegra hasn't dated anyone since that asshole last year."

"At least I'm not the only one in a dry spell." Bree found working with men all day had the opposite reaction one might suspect. She heard dirty jokes, complaints about wives and girlfriends, and saw enough spitting to fill the Mississippi River. When she got home at night, the last thing she wanted was to be with more men.

"You know my history wasn't stellar until I met Drake. Just don't let Mom think she had a hand in it or she'll start matchmaking again."

"Had a hand in what?" Drake, Elle's tech genius fiancé, asked as he walked up with two mimosas.

"Hooking you two up," Bree said before taking a sip and coughing. "This isn't a mimosa."

Drake smiled and she heard Elle sigh with pleasure. Ugh, she was going to have to be around this all the time now. "Vodka. I saw you with Aunt Flory earlier." Okay, so maybe she could put up with mushy stuff. Drake was going to be a pretty awesome brother-in-law.

"We were just watching that," Elle said with a nod to Finn and Allegra. "Do you know anything about it?"

Drake shrugged his broad shoulders. "They're just friends. Allegra helped Finn a lot when he was putting together the proposal to buy the sports agency. Finn mentioned she was recommending a couple of big-name models to Simpson Entertainment Agency, too."

"And I go to Finn's gym with her in the morning, but I don't see anything unusual going on between them." Elle lowered her voice. "Don't let Aunt Flory hear us, but look at Mary and Phillip. Since they got together, it's like she's a new person. Before she moped around the office and would never do much for us. But now she's killing it in the PR department and looks so happy and confident."

"Phillip, too. He's pulled back some of his outrageous behavior and is suddenly using words like *future* and *I'll check with Mary*," Drake joked.

"I'm so happy for them." Bree was interrupted by her phone. "Marcus?"

"Marcus?" Margaret's head popped up from across the room.

"He's my site manager," Bree hissed as she put her hand over the phone. "It's Saturday. What's going on?"

Bree listened to Marcus and hung up with a sigh. Apparently it wasn't only her car that had been vandalized.

Chapter Three

L ogan had worked without sleep for almost two days. His secretary was about to kill him, and he was about to kill the next person who dared talk to him. But he'd gotten two weeks' worth of work done in two days and was back at Heathrow Airport. This was the first time he was looking forward to an eight-and-a-half-hour flight.

Dragging his carry-on behind him, he walked down the gate and found his seat in Business Class. He was asleep before the door was closed. Dreams of telling the spoiled Simpson heir to go to hell filled his head. While he didn't know Mr. Simpson, he'd heard all about him building up casinos in Europe with his inheritance. And he'd be stupid if he hadn't heard of Elle Simpson. Apparently she wrangled her brother in from Europe. When Logan was in Dubai, he'd heard that Simpson had left for some build in Atlanta. He'd already reworked the Atlanta corporate center plans more times than he could remember and Mr. Simpson was about to learn that he couldn't get everything he wanted.

Marcus stood with his hands on his jean-clad hips waiting for Bree. She parked on the street and popped the trunk to the sports car Reid let her borrow. As soon as she got out of the car, Marcus walked toward her.

"I don't know the extent of the damage yet. I've called the police and the crew. As soon as the police get here and document everything, the crew will start cleaning it up," Marcus said with a hard edge to his voice.

Bree rarely saw this side of him. Marcus was always calm and collected. Bree slipped off her wedges and grabbed her boots from the trunk. "Let's go see the extent of the damage while we wait for everyone to show up." She reached in again and pulled out her pink hard hat.

"It starts here. The office is ransacked." Bree stomped across the dirt and gravel to where the office windows were smashed and hot pink spray paint covered the outside. The words *slut* and *whore* were written along the walls of the trailer.

Bree stepped into the office and wanted to cry. Papers were everywhere. Desks were broken. Cabinets lay in splinters around the room. "Were you able to save anything?"

"Everything was destroyed except for the papers I had at home. Luckily, those were the ones we need the most. I'd also saved all the computer files to an external hard drive. So really, it's just a fright to look at, but it won't ruin us."

"Thank goodness. When Mallory gets home, I'll have her increase security and see if she can do something to help." Bree paused and let out a slow breath.

She knew that Elle would want to know, but Bree didn't want to admit she had failed her big sister. Elle wouldn't get mad; Bree knew that. But it didn't mean admitting defeat would be welcome. Elle would become involved and the last thing she wanted was for her to be the target of those mysterious green letters. She needed to make sure she took control of the situation and handled it with competence to protect her sister.

"What else was damaged?" she asked.

"This is as far as I went. I can see spray paint on some of the equipment but thought I better call you first."

"Let's go take a look." Bree set her jaw and focused all her attention on calculating the cost of the damage.

As she walked around the equipment, she saw members of the construction crew arriving. Soon police would come, but she had a feeling they wouldn't be fast about it. Whoever was behind this had enough power to feel as if they were invincible, which usually meant they had a police or government contact.

Marcus tapped her on the shoulder as they took in the damage outside the building. "Police are finally here. It only took them an hour and a half," he said with disgust.

"Ah, but that is good news," Bree smiled as she waved to the uniformed officers and started to head their way.

"How?"

"Because that narrows my list of suspects to two. Only Trevor Marion and Jeff Henderson have those kinds of contacts. They inadvertently gave themselves away. Now we just have to figure out which one is behind this." Bree stopped her explanation when some of the workers approached.

"What should we do, Bree?" Al, one of the workers, asked.

"As soon as the police wrap up, we'll start cleaning up. I'm so sorry to call you all in today."

"It's okay. It gets us all riled up when this happens. Do you know who it was yet?"

"Not yet, but I have an idea. I'd better go talk to the police." Bree and Marcus headed toward the police officers who were taking their sweet time getting out of the cruiser.

"You the senior site manager?" the older officer asked Marcus while ignoring Bree.

"That's right," Marcus said as he drew himself up. "And this is Miss Bree Simpson, the vice president of Simpson Steel and Construction."

The police officer ignored her again. "What seems to be the problem?"

"The problem?" Bree asked incredulously. "You don't see the spray paint everywhere or the broken windows?"

The police officer never looked at her. He slid his pad into his back pocket and addressed Marcus. "Probably just some construction hijinks. You know how it is."

"Al," Bree yelled. The group of workers stopped talking and big Al stepped forward. "Yes?"

Al was a loveable big teddy bear who also happened to be the size of a bear. He was at least three hundred and fifty pounds and six feet seven inches tall. More importantly, he could be very intimidating.

"This officer here believes all this damage was just construction site hijinks. Did you or any of the boys do this?" Bree called out. The men straightened to their full height and stared daggers at the officer whose collar suddenly felt tight by the way he pulled at it.

"No, ma'am. We'd never do something like that. You're the best boss we've ever had, and I dare anyone to say otherwise," Al said as he lumbered toward them. The other men all crossed their arms over their broad chests and nodded their agreement.

"Good, I'm glad we've got that cleared up. Al, why don't you take this officer around the site and make sure he documents all the damage."

"I'll be happy to. Officer?" The officer gave an audible

swallow and followed Al to the offices.

"I'm going to have a look inside. I hope they didn't compromise the integrity of the structure," Bree sighed.

"I'll come with you," Marcus said as they walked across the site toward the building.

Logan tossed his bags on the bed of the hotel and stepped to the window. Opening the curtains, he looked at the construction site he was here to visit. A pink hard hat stood out along with the hot pink spray paint that seemed to cover the site. It looks like Mr. Simpson was having some problems on site. Probably upset workers. If Mr. Simpson was such a pain in the ass to him, he couldn't imagine what he put his workers through.

He looked around and saw the expensive sports car and the man standing next to the woman in the pink hardhat and bright blue sundress. She must be his trophy wife. Figures he'd drag some hot young thing along to the construction site with him. Men like him liked to show their virility through the women on their arms. Logan would deal with this later. He turned away from the problem and stripped off his shirt. A hot shower was needed before he dealt with B. Simpson.

Fifteen minutes later, Logan combed his wet hair away from his face and stepped into a pair of jeans. He looked back out the window as he tied his shoes and watched Mr. Simpson and his trophy wife with her "cute" pink hat head into the half-built building. Logan started to button his white shirt when an explosion rocked the hotel.

He grabbed the windowsill and watched in horror as part of the corporate center crashed to the ground. A cloud of dust left him unable to see anything on the site. Slowly it cleared enough for him to see fire lapping at the steel, smoke billowing into the sky, and men standing in shock as they stared at the collapsing building.

Chapter Four

L ogan was out of his room and racing down the stairs before he knew it. He shoved open the door and pushed his way through the crowd watching the fire from the lobby. Dust swarmed his eyes and strangled his throat.

Traffic had stopped, and some people were pressing their faces to their windows while a brave few were standing stunned in their open doors. Logan had to leap over the hood of a car to make it across the street. He ran past an officer radioing in for help. The smoke was burning his lungs, and the heat of the fire was intense. He ripped off his shirt and wrapped it around his nose and mouth.

A big man was weeping as the other workers were yelling, "Boss?" into the inferno.

"Are they alive?" Logan yelled to the big man.

"We don't know. Oh, God. Oh, God," he wept.

Logan pushed through the wall of workers now spraying the fire with water hoses and whatever fire extinguishers they could find.

"Spray me down!"

The man with the hose looked at him with confusion. "Spray me down, now! I'm going in," Logan yelled right before he was hit with the cold water.

As soon as he was wet, he turned toward the building

and took it in. He ascertained the best point of entry and remembered it was around where Mr. Simpson and his wife went in. He felt the fire lick at his arms and bare chest as he ran through the open door and into the remains of the building.

Logan had to raise his arm to cover his forehead as he looked around. The heat was searing and the smoke burned his eyes. He made his way slowly forward as he scanned the floor looking for the couple.

At the center of the building he saw the hole caused by the explosion. He followed the crevice to where two steel beams had collapsed. He saw the man. He wasn't moving and the way the beam was lying across him, Logan feared he wasn't alive.

The fire was so deafening he didn't hear the person with the fire extinguisher until white foam covered his back. He looked up and saw the big man who had been crying.

"Oh my God! Is he alive?"

"I don't know!" Logan had to shout back.

Logan crawled forward and winced at the way Mr. Simpson's leg was twisted under the beam. He placed a hand at the base of his neck. It was faint, but there was a flicker of a pulse.

"He's alive, but not for long." Logan tried to lift the beam, but couldn't. The fire was closing in on them. "Help me!"

The big man bent down and when they nodded to each other, they lifted with all their strength. The beam barely moved, but it was enough. "Get him out," the man grunted as his muscles bulged.

Logan didn't hesitate. He let go of the beam and grabbed B. Simpson by his shoulders. He pulled with all he had. The adrenaline pumping through his body helped as he pulled the man free of the beam. The big man dropped the beam as soon as B. Simpson was clear. His thick arms shook as he looked down at the man. "Are you sure he's alive?"

"No, I'm not." Logan felt for a pulse and shook his head. "Can you carry him out? I'm going to look for the woman."

"You have to save her. Please." The man bent over and scooped B. Simpson into his arms, then disappeared into the smoke.

Logan coughed and pressed his damp shirt to his mouth. If she was in here with her husband, then she should be near. Crawling on his hands and knees, he started searching the area. He found her lying on her stomach only feet from where her husband had been. Part of the ceiling and the edge of a beam were on the ground next to her shattered hard hat.

Logan's heart plummeted. She's taken a hit to the head from falling debris. It didn't look good. Her bright blue dress stood out against the black smoke. Her strawberry blonde hair was fanned out around her head. She looked like an angel. Logan felt tears welling for this woman he didn't even know.

Crawling to her, he pushed her hair back from her face. His fingers left a trail of soot along her soft cheek as he pressed his fingers to her neck to confirm what he saw. Logan almost jumped back when he felt the strong pulse under his fingers. "Mrs. Simpson," he yelled. "Can you hear me?"

The woman didn't move. The fire crackled and some more of the building crashed down not fifteen feet from them. He rolled her over on her back and slid his arms under her shoulders and knees. "Come on, Mrs. Simpson. Live for me," Logan murmured as he rounded his shoulders, trying to protect her as much as possible from the heat and debris. He used his knee to keep her upright as he took his wet shirt and laid it over her. He lifted her into his arms and realized the cleared area he'd come through was shrinking with the growing flames.

Logan tucked the woman to his chest and ran. He leaped over debris and dodged more when a section of the ceiling fell. Through the dancing flames, he could see movement. He could hear yelling. And then he felt the blessed spray of the hose. The men had seen him and were trying to make an opening through the flames for him to escape. The fire hissed in anger at the water, and Logan jumped.

Bree couldn't remember being so hot before. She was from the South. She was no wimp when it came to hot, humid summer days. But this was different. It felt as if her body was literally on fire and her hair was melting. Someone was calling her, but the escape into the darkness was more appealing. Anything to get away from this heat.

All too soon, though, she was dragged from the darkness. She was floating. Was she dead? Bree tried to open her eyes, but as soon as she did they burned so badly she slammed them shut. All she saw in that split second was the very blurry image of a shirtless man holding her and flames surrounding them. Oh God, she was going to hell and being carried there by a really hot angel of death. The darkness came again and she fought it. She heard screaming and felt the fire engulfing her.

"Hang on. I've got you."

The encouraging words with the deep Southern accent soothed her. He wasn't an angel of death. She felt the strength of him protecting her. Bree floated back into darkness, knowing she was safe.

Logan burst through the flames and was immediately covered with wet towels. The fire department roared onto the scene. Ambulances were fighting through traffic and tearing into the construction site. One lone ambulance sped away from the scene. Thank goodness, Mr. Simpson was on the way to the hospital. The lights flashing and the horn blaring told Logan he was still alive, but barely.

"He found her!" some of the men yelled as they encircled him. It was obvious from the affection of the crew they liked their boss's wife. "Is she alive?"

"Get that ambulance! She's unconscious and sustained a head injury." Logan refused to relinquish his hold on her. Holding her tight, he willed the beautiful woman to live.

The men waved down the nearest ambulance. The paramedics leapt down and peppered him with questions.

"She was hit on the head by falling debris and possibly a steel beam. Her hard hat was shattered by the impact. She hasn't regained consciousness."

"Are you her husband?" the paramedic asked as an IV was put in and a mask covered her face.

"No. Her husband was in that first ambulance. He pushed her out of the way. He was trying to save her." Logan watched as she was loaded into the ambulance.

"Then you'd better come with us. He's not expected to make it."

Logan didn't bother to tell them he didn't know anything more, but he couldn't imagine leaving her to suffer all by herself. When she woke, he would tell her how her husband was a hero.

Logan stayed out of the way as the paramedics worked on
Mrs. Simpson. She wasn't responding and she wasn't
waking up. Her heart rate started to slow and with a yell to
the driver, the ambulance sped through traffic. The line
showing her heart rate started to straighten and then there
was the ominous sound of a flatline.

"She's coding!" the EMT shouted.

Logan couldn't tear his eyes from her. She couldn't die.
She was too young, too full of life, just an hour ago. He
watched in horror as the two EMTs worked as a fluid pair.
One cut away her sundress as the other prepped the
paddles and handed them over. They were slapped onto
her chest in fewer than ten seconds.

"Clear." Her body jerked and the monitor beeped to
life.

"She's back!" the EMT told the driver. His partner
grabbed the radio and told them their location and her
status.

After the shock, her arm had fallen off the gurney.
Logan tentatively reached out and took her small, delicate
hand into his. He wouldn't leave her until she was safe. Did
she have family? Did she have children who had to be told
their father was most likely dead and their mother's life lay
in the balance? Would she have someone to take care of
her? The overwhelming need to protect this woman
consumed him. He was surprised to find it was he who
wanted to be the one to care for her. Guilt nagged at him.
This was someone else's wife and he wanted to be there for
her. Ten years of distancing himself and here he was willing
a women he'd never met to live, knowing he'd have to
leave her to mourn the death of her husband.

The ambulance came to a stop by the emergency room and the back doors flung open. Men and women in different-colored scrubs were peppering the EMTs with questions as they unloaded Mrs. Simpson from the ambulance and rushed her into the hospital.

"Sir! What's her name? Do you know her blood type?" a nurse asked as they hurried to follow the doctors inside.

"Mrs. Simpson. That's all I know. Her husband was just brought in. How is he?"

"He wasn't breathing when we got to him. They rushed him into surgery. That's all I know. Wait here and someone will be out with an update. If you know any of her family, now's the time to call them."

Then Logan was alone.

Chapter Five

An irritating beeping drew Bree out of the sexiest dream she'd ever had. She had been rolling around naked with her angel rescuer on a fluffy white cloud while lightning struck all around. As her eyes fluttered, she heard voices fill with excitement. Bright lights blinded her and everything was blurry. Maybe she had died and this was heaven. No, it couldn't be. In heaven, she wouldn't have the worst headache imaginable. Bree fought with her eyes as she tried to get them into focus.

"Ma'am. You're in the hospital. You've been in an accident, but you're safe now. Can you open your eyes for me?"

Bree cringed at the light and suddenly it was gone. The relief made her sigh with pleasure. She blinked again and focused on the figure standing at the foot of the bed. Slowly his two bodies morphed together and she gasped. It was her angel.

"Are you all right, Mrs. Simpson?"

"Yes. What happened?"

"There was an explosion. Do you remember it?" the doctor asked.

Bree closed her eyes and thought back to the engagement party, the message from Marcus, the corrupt police officer, the damage to the building, and then the earth fell out from under her feet.

"Oh my God — how is he? Where is he? He pushed me out of the way when the ceiling collapsed." Bree was frantic. What happened to Marcus? He had saved her life. She felt cold all of a sudden. Her body started to shake as it remembered the explosion, the impact, and the darkness.

Suddenly there was warmth. It was in her hand and slowly spread up her arm. "Take a breath, Mrs. Simpson. It's okay. You're safe."

Bree opened her eyes and focused on the large hand covering hers. The mysterious angel's slate-colored eyes drew her in. Her body stopped shaking and she drew in a slow breath.

"Your husband is alive. That's what's important right now." Bree let out a shaky breath as his deep voice washed over her. There was something so sure about his voice that no matter what he said, she would believe him. Marcus was alive and that was all that mattered. Why did they think he was her husband, though? She was about to ask when the doctor cut in.

"He lost a leg and is pretty banged up. He's still in critical condition and it's going to be a tough forty-eight hours for him. It doesn't look good, Mrs. Simpson, and I need you to prepare for the worst." The doctor looked down at his cell phone. "I have to go to surgery. The nurse can answer any questions for you and we'll try to get you to see your husband after you rest some. However, I would advise you see him sooner rather than later. I'm sorry."

Bree gasped. Marcus had lost his leg and now he might die because he saved her. He had thrown himself under the beam when he pushed her out of the way. Tears fell from her eyes. The pain made each tear hurt as it rolled down her cheeks.

"Do you have a phone?" she asked her angel, who she could only guess was a doctor. He looked like it with his dark brown hair and those eyes. He looked tired and scruffy, just like any medical professional after a twelve-hour shift.

"Of course."

Logan pulled out his cell phone and turned it on. He swallowed hard as he handed her the phone and their fingers touched. *I'm going to hell*, he thought. He couldn't control his emotions with someone else's wife. Someone who was fighting for his life right now. What kind of horrible man was he? Logan fought the urge to wrap her in his arms and instead pulled a chair to the side of her bed.

He'd been floored when her teal eyes had fluttered open. When she'd looked at him and it was like a sucker punch to the stomach. He closed his eyes as she dialed the phone and chastised himself.

"It's me. There's been an explosion. Yes, I'm okay. I have a bad concussion. My hard hat saved me." Mrs. Simpson paused as Logan imagined whoever she called digesting this information.

"No. He's critical. He pushed me out of the way and a beam landed on him. They had to amputate his leg."

Logan slid from the room and waved down a nurse. "She's really upset. I don't know how she's going to rest."

The nurse nodded and told him she'd take care of it. When Logan came back into the room, Bree had set his phone on the corner of the bed and was silently crying. Her shoulders shook as tears streaked her face.

"Thank you."

Logan sat down and took her hand in his. "Have you made all the calls you need?"

"Yes. My sister will call everyone else in the family.

What am I going to do? How can I sit here when he's . . . he's . . . oh God! It's all my fault," she cried.

The woman's body was wracked with sobs and Logan felt completely helpless. "Ah, here's your nurse. She's going to give you a little something . . ."

Logan watched the nurse check Bree's eyes before injecting some medicine into her line. "Her eyes aren't dilated, which is good. This is a small dose to help her relax. She'll be up in an hour or so."

"Thank you," Logan murmured as the drugs took effect. The tears slowed and her eyelids closed with a flutter. When the nurse left the room, Logan scooted his chair closer and placed his hand on hers. He didn't know how, but he'd find a way to help her.

Bree struggled against the drugs but eventually let them take over. The darkness welcomed her once again, but the peace didn't last long. Memories bombarded her in fragmented flashes: talking with Marcus, the explosion, being pushed, the hit, total darkness, and then him. He was there. He had carried her to safety.

Bree's eyes shot open. He was still there. Her rescuer. He had to be the EMT who came in to find her. She remembered him carrying her out of the fire. Remembered him holding her hand in the ambulance.

"The doctor came in with an update. Mr. Simpson is still in critical condition and they have him in a medically induced coma. He's also on a breathing tube. I'm sorry, it's not looking good," the angel doctor said as he squeezed her hand.

"Mr. Simpson?" Bree asked, her mind still foggy with sleep medicine. "He's dead."

"Don't think like that. He has a lot of fight left in him."

"No, he doesn't. He's dead. Mr. Simpson is dead and buried, may he rest in peace. If he comes back, then he'll be a zombie and I don't think that would be good." Bree shook her head. Why were they talking about her father? He had died eight years ago.

"You're distraught . . ."

"Get out of my way!"

Logan looked up as a golden-haired beauty ran into the room with a nurse trailing after her.

"You can't be in here, miss," the nurse said, a bit annoyed at having to chase the woman down.

"I'm her sister and you better be prepared to drag me kicking and screaming if you expect me to leave."

Logan hid a laugh behind a cough. This woman wouldn't take any shit. He felt sorry for the nurse as Mrs. Simpson's sister stared her down. The nurse spun around and left with the threat of getting the doctor.

"How are you?" she asked, hurrying to her sister's side.

"Tired. They gave me some medicine to calm me down. And my head hurts worse than spending an afternoon with Aunt Flory. But I was told the hard hat saved me from worse."

The sister sat on the bed and put her arm around Mrs. Simpson. Logan looked at them as they hugged. They looked very similar. Both were around the same height and build and had the same smooth jaw lines and high cheekbones. The only real difference was Mrs. Simpson had lighter hair and deeper eyes.

"I've sent for Mallory. Security will be here any minute. I want you safe while you recover."

Logan saw the nurse in a heated talk with the doctor through the glass door. Seconds later, the doctor pushed open the door to the room. "This is the ICU; you can't be in here," he said, addressing the newcomer.

"I'm her sister Elle. Of course I can be in here."

"Miss Simpson?" the doctor asked with wide eyes.

"Yes?" both sisters responded.

"I'm sorry, Miss Simpson. We didn't know. We had your sister registered as just Mrs. Simpson and I didn't put it together," the doctor flushed.

Why was the doctor suddenly sucking up so much? Logan looked back and forth between them. Wait, if Elle was also a Simpson . . .

"This is my sister Bree. I'll be out in a minute to register her completely," Elle stated with such authority that Logan had his answer.

"B. Simpson," he murmured with wonder as the doctor left.

Elle's sharp eyes turned on him. "And you are?" she asked with such control that it sent shivers down Logan's back.

"Oh, this is the doctor who rescued me." Bree smiled as she looked at him. Logan felt like a hero when she looked at him like that. He couldn't tear his gaze from hers but had no choice when Elle launched herself at him.

"Thank you so much. I don't know how to thank you. You saved my sister's life," Elle said with emotion causing her voice to crack as she wrapped Logan up in a hug.

So, the ice queen wasn't so icy after all. She was just worried about her sister, and quite frankly, it surprised him. In families with as much money as the Simpsons, siblings usually tended to feud. His sure did. No one was happy sharing the wealth, but this appeared to be a very different type of family.

Bree looked up at him with such warmth that Logan felt as if he were the king of the world. "I'm so sorry. You saved me and comforted me, and I never asked your name."

Logan answered without hesitation as he basked her in smile. "Logan. Logan Ward."

Suddenly her smile slipped. Her face grew pink and those warm teal eyes turned hard as stone. "Logan Ward!" she screamed.

Chapter Six

Men in black suits piled through the door right as a pillow hit Logan in the face. The security Elle had mentioned hit first and asked questions later. With a whoosh of air leaving his lungs, Logan was brought to the ground.

"Do you know how much time and money you've wasted? And now my site manager is fighting for his life. Tell me this, are you working with them? Are you trying to ruin me and this project?"

From his place on the floor, Logan looked up to see Bree standing on the bed and trying to leap down while Elle worked hard to get her to sit back down.

"What's going on here?" Bree whipped around too fast and turned white. She saw the woman standing at the door just before she lost her balance. A scream lodged in her throat as Elle grabbed for her.

Logan saw Bree's arm pinwheel as she fell backward off the bed. He pushed off the stunned security guards staring at her bare bottom as Elle grabbed the front of the hospital gown to try to save her from falling. The gown didn't have a chance. The flimsy ties broke and a naked Bree fell right into Logan's outstretched arms.

"Oh, I need to try that next time I'm in the hospital. Who can ask for more than to be naked in a hot guy's arms?

Well, I guess it could be better if he were naked, too."

Logan tore his eyes away from Bree's perfect breasts and saw an old woman with a walker that read *I like men the way I like pictures . . . well hung* standing by the door with a smile on her face. Maybe he needed to see a doctor; this couldn't be real. But then the woman who looked like an older version of Elle and Bree rushed inside the room along with a younger version of herself and two men.

"Oh jeez. I can't un-see that," one of the men said as he covered his eyes.

"It's okay, Drake. I got this," the other man said with anger radiating off him. "Put my sister down this moment. Whoever you are, you have a lot of explaining to do."

Bree had closed her eyes, hoping the fall from the bed wouldn't hurt too badly but landing naked in Logan Ward's arms was even worse. Why couldn't the floor have opened up and swallowed her instead? Those strong arms she remembered carrying her through the fire had reached out and caught her. He instinctively pulled her into him as he cradled her naked body against his hard chest.

She'd meant to read him the riot act, exposed or not, but then she'd looked up into a set of very appreciative slate-blue eyes scanning her body. The desire she saw there took her breath away. Whatever kind of moment they had was ruined as soon as she heard Shirley, followed by the fact her soon-to-be brother-in-law had just seen a whole lot of her bare butt. However, that was nothing compared to her *brother* now trying to rip her out of Logan's arms. She was entangled in a game of naked tug-of-war with a roomful of people watching.

"Put her down!"

"I will not!"

"She's my sister and I'll kill you if that finger moves one inch closer to her breast."

"Oh for the love of Pete. Reid, cover your sister with a blanket. You, whoever you are, put my daughter down right this instant." Her mother clapped her hands and suddenly the room bounded into action. A blanket appeared and Logan set her down on the bed before security rushed to grab him again.

"That's enough," Margaret said with a wave of her hand. The guards backed down but didn't leave the room. "Now, would someone tell me what is going on?"

"He's Logan Ward."

"She's B. Simpson."

"He saved her."

Bree, Logan, and Elle all said at the same time.

"Oh, I think I broke a hip. Help, help, I need saving," Shirley said with a wink toward Logan.

Bree shook her head and enjoyed Logan's unease under Shirley's roaming eyes. "He's the architect who's been delaying my build. I think he's colluding with another builder to delay the construction and ruin the build in order to get me fired."

"I thought the architect was British," Allegra said as she looked Logan over.

Bree nodded her agreement. She thought he was, too.

"I'm from Charleston, South Carolina. I went to school in London for architecture and was picked up immediately upon graduation by the Clarke Group. And I'm not the one delaying the project. You are. It's exactly as I suspected. Some rich heiress wants to play designer and you can't make up your mind!"

Bree, along with everyone else in the room, sucked in some air at the insult. Bree felt her face turn red and she tried to launch herself at Logan again, but Reid pushed her back into bed. "Stay!" he ordered.

Allegra stomped across the room in her nude designer heels and beautiful green dress. In a move faster than Bree could blink, she smashed her perfectly manicured fist into Logan's handsome face.

"Allegra Simpson!" Margaret yelled.

"Yes, Mother?" Allegra asked sweetly as she shook her hand.

"Where did you learn that?" Margaret asked, completely ignoring Logan's look of shock at having received a split lip at the hands of one of the sweetest Southern belles you'd ever meet.

"Finn taught me. He didn't like me to be in all those warehouse districts alone," Allegra shrugged.

"I knew I liked that boy," Margaret smiled. "Now, I think it's time you leave, Mr. Ward. My daughter needs her rest."

The clearing of a throat had everyone turning to the door. "I'm sorry," the man in a cheap gray suit said with an air of pissed-off authority. "But I need to speak with Mr. Ward and Miss Simpson. I'm Detective Gruber and I have some questions for you both."

Elle took hold of her sister's hand and Reid stepped forward. "We aren't going anywhere. If you want to talk to our sister, you can talk with us here."

Bree already knew what was going to happen. It was the same as the police officer at the work site this morning. Whoever had blown up the site had the police, or at least certain officers, in their pocket. The look on Detective Gruber's face was enough to let her know nothing was going to happen with the case. Elle and Reid just didn't realize it yet.

"That sounds like a good idea," Margaret said as she looked Detective Gruber over. "We'll let you all talk while I make a phone call to Agent Wallace at the Secret Service. He's a close friend of ours and I want him to get the Feds to look over the scene to ensure it was not an act of terrorism. Which I believe falls under federal jurisdiction, does it not?" Margaret asked sweetly as she gave Detective Gruber a slow smile before herding everyone else out the door.

Mallory's bodyguards stepped outside the door. Logan could see their wide shoulders through the small window as they took up their positions for the night.

Detective Gruber pushed his glasses up his nose. While he might have been an attractive man in his prime, now in his fifties, he looked like he lifted the more beer cans than weights. His eyes were a little too close together, giving him the overall appearance of a weasel.

"Miss Simpson, with all due respect, I've looked over the crime scene. It appears to be an accident."

Logan had a hard time controlling his reaction. Accident? That wasn't an accident. He'd seen the fire and the site of explosion — that was no accident. It was a bomb. Before he could say anything, though, Reid was already jumping in.

"Accident?" he said with surprise. "How so?"

"Looks like a generator exploded. Miss Simpson probably made them leave it on so she could have more lighting while she went inside to do whatever it was she was doing." Turning to Bree, he smiled as if she were a child. "Your heels could have punctured something or you switched something on not realizing what it was."

Elle opened her mouth, but Bree put a hand on her arm to quiet her down. "You're right, Detective. You know us women. Always walking around construction sites in high heels and playing with switches. Why did I even bother getting a dual degree in engineering and chemistry? Elle, I'm sorry I wasted so much of the family's time and money on getting my master's in engineering as well."

Logan rocked back on his heels and smiled. She was spunky; he'd give her that. He was also man enough to admit when he was wrong, and he was definitely wrong about the infamous "B. Simpson". As soon as this asshole left, he'd apologize for thinking she was a ditzy heiress.

"Why don't you do me a favor, Detective? It would save us a bunch of trouble. Go back to the man who paid you to lie about this explosion and tell him I'm coming after him. If he thinks I like big hammers, wait until he sees the hammer I'm going to bring down on him. I won't stop there, either. After he's in jail, I'm coming after all of you he's paid off to do his dirty work. Is it worth your pension, Detective? Your freedom?" Bree stared him down and Logan's mind started churning. There was a lot more going on here than he thought.

"I think it's time you leave, Detective," Elle said, stepping forward to stand shoulder to shoulder with her brother.

Detective Gruber slammed his little notebook shut and glared. He was a bully, and he was used to people backing down. Too bad Bree wasn't going to give in. She dealt with worse on a daily basis and she was going to get to the bottom of this, no matter what. She'd be damned if she cared who she took down along the way. Gruber must have realized it as his jaw tightened in anger. He eventually turned and walked out the door without saying a word.

"What did you mean, Bree? What haven't you been telling me?" Elle asked the second the door closed.

Bree let out a sigh and lay back down in bed. Her head

was throbbing. Her body seemed to melt into the bed and her eyes were starting to droop. "I've been receiving threats. They all come on green paper. First it was about the site, but then they turned into threats against me if I didn't step down. And then construction kept being delayed because of Mr. Ward. And then things started happening at the site and this morning my car was vandalized. Then when Marcus called about the vandalizing of the construction site—" Bree choked up. "Will someone please check on Marcus?"

"I'm sure Mom will take good care of him." Elle's phone beeped and she read the message. "Good, Mallory is almost here. I had to pull her from a job on Hung Island."

"Where are the notes, sis?" Reid asked.

"At the office," Bree said tiredly.

"I'll go get them," Reid said before he bent over and placed a kiss on Bree's forehead. "I love you, sis."

"I love you, too."

Logan watched as Reid looked torn. It was clear he didn't want to leave but knew the faster he moved, the faster they could get the evidence and get to the bottom of this. He was interested in seeing the notes, too.

"Bree, Miss Simpson—" Logan started. He didn't know what to call her. He hadn't wanted to personalize her when she was B. Simpson and he thought she was a pain in his ass. But now, he knew he'd been wrong. He'd saved her, held her naked in his arms, and no matter what, he was involved in more ways than he cared to admit.

The door opened and a blonde bombshell interrupted him. She wore tight black leather pants and a blood-red, silk tank top with matching stilettos. A strand of pearls lay delicately across her throat. Big blue eyes took in every corner of the room in seconds.

"Mallory, I'm so glad you're here," Bree said as she yawned and held out her hand.

Mallory hurried across the room and took her hand. "Ah, Mr. Ward. Nice of you to decide to show up finally."

"I'm at a disadvantage. You seem to know me, but I don't know you," Logan said. He couldn't decide what to make of this woman who looked like the perfect lady, except for the edge that she fought to conceal beneath the pearls. Whoever she was, she was not what she appeared.

"Mallory Westin, owner of Westin Security."

"Did the cameras pick up anything?" Bree asked as the rest of her family made their way back into the cramped room.

"There were cameras?" Elle and Logan asked at the same time.

"We installed them while Bree went to England," Mallory told them as she pulled up a video on her tablet. "This is all we got."

Everyone leaned forward and watched a man in black with a ski mask enter the building. He pulled out a large device and turned it on before hiding it beneath some plastic sheets. The angle changed and they watched as he snuck out the back of the site and disappeared in the night. The screen went black until images of Bree and Marcus came on. Mallory pressed pause.

"That's it," Mallory said as she lowered the tablet.

"No, you have more on there. I want to see it," Bree said with a shaky voice.

"It's nothing that will help you," Mallory said softly.

"I don't care. I *have* to see it," Bree demanded.

Mallory looked at Elle who gave a silent nod in agreement. Mallory lifted the tablet and pressed Play. They watched as Bree and Marcus walked deeper into the building, then the screen went bright white and then black as the camera was taken out in the explosion. Elle gasped and Logan shot a look at Bree. She was staring at the screen in silence. The screen turned to the camera in the parking lot facing the building.

At first they couldn't see anything because of the dust, but then flames and the chaos began to appear. Elle cried silently and Bree didn't breathe as they watched Logan running through the crowd and ripping off his shirt before disappearing into the flames. Al was next, rushing in with a fire extinguisher as the other workers ran for more hoses. Soon Al appeared carrying Marcus and the first ambulance slid to a stop.

"Who's that?" Elle asked, pointing at the entrance of the building.

"That is Mr. Ward," Mallory told her.

Elle's eyes went wide as Logan leapt through the flames protecting Bree with his body. "I thanked you before, Mr. Ward, but . . ." Elle gave up on fighting the tears and hugged Logan as they dripped onto his shoulder.

"Why do I feel as if I keep coming into the room at the wrong time?"

"Drake, he saved Bree. He . . . he fought flames for her and protected her," Elle cried.

"Then it's a pleasure to peel my fiancée off of you. I'm Drake Charles and I, too, can't thank you enough for saving my almost sister-in-law." Drake pulled Elle into his arms as she continued to shake with tears.

Logan shook his hand and even noticed Mallory turning away for a second to collect herself. But it was Bree who had his attention. She hadn't moved. Her face was white and her eyes in a far-off place.

"Logan Ward," he said absently to Drake as he moved

to stand near the bed.

Bree turned slowly and looked up at him. "You risked your life for me? Why?"

"You're worth fighting fire for," he said seriously. "I saw you from my hotel window and I can't explain it . . ."

"I think this is where we give you two a moment," Drake smiled and gently pushed Elle from the room.

Mallory and the rest of Bree's family followed closely behind. With tears in her eyes, Margret rose on her toes and gave Logan a silent kiss on the cheek. The look in her eyes conveyed a bevy of emotions and Logan understood them all as he gave her a gentle smile. And then they were alone. Logan suddenly felt very self-conscious as Bree looked at him.

"I think it's time we talked, Mr. Ward."

Chapter Seven

Bree looked up at Logan Ward in disbelief. She'd spent the last months thinking of him as the bad guy. Someone who did what he'd done wouldn't be out to destroy her. She watched as he nervously stepped closer and took a seat on the chair next to the bed.

His dark hair was slightly wavy and pushed back. Stubble was starting to appear along his strong jawline and the bottom of an intricate tribal tattoo peeked out from under the sleeve of his borrowed scrubs. He was definitely not what she was expecting.

Bree took a deep breath and did something she hated more than her yearly Pap smear. "I'm sorry. I was wrong about you." His gray-blue eyes widened a bit in amusement and he took her hand in his.

"I was wrong about you, too. Let's start over, shall we?" His lips quirked and Bree stared at his mouth for a moment before realizing she needed to answer.

"I'm Bree Simpson. It's a pleasure to meet you, Mr. Ward."

"I think you should call me Logan." His eyes twinkled in amusement again before turning serious. They deepened then, turning grayer as his warm hand tightened slightly over hers. "Bree, what's going on with this project?"

"I think someone is trying to take the job away from

me. The threats made it clear he was in the construction business and wants me to step down and clean house when I go. When I refused, it started escalating. The police are brushing me off and that actually helped me. I was telling Marcus right before . . . before the explosion . . .," Bree took a deep breath and tried to fight the tears back, ". . . that I had narrowed it down to four people who were strong and dirty enough to do these things. But with the intervention of the police, I have it narrowed down to two. Trevor Marion and Jeff Henderson. Have you heard of either of them?"

Logan shook his head. "But one thing I think we need to clear up is the delays. I submitted the final plans a week before they were due. What was with all the angry messages wanting the final prints?"

Bree snatched her hand from his and crossed her arms. "Final plans? I have six sets of final plans. I keep getting emails from your secretary about more plans coming."

"Well, when you keep ordering changes, I have to keep sending revisions," Logan shot back.

"But I'm *not* sending changes. It was perfect the first time."

Logan leaned back and looked at Bree. "You're not asking for the changes?"

"No."

"Then who is?" Logan wondered aloud.

"Well, who is calling you asking for them?"

"No one. They are coming from my boss. He said he was friends with someone handling the corporate center project. I thought he meant you," Logan said as his mind started racing.

"It's not me. But you know these building types. I may own a large share, but I'm only one of around twenty people. However, in our contract I have total control over the build. So I was right—someone is trying to delay it. If I don't meet the timeline, then I lose control of the build and the other owners would be able to pick who they want to head it up. It's a deal worth hundreds of millions of dollars," Bree told him.

"It's all about the money. The funny thing is these guys probably have more of it than they'd ever need." Logan shook his head in wonder. He didn't envy Bree or her family. If they were actually as nice as they seemed, even the sister who punched him, they probably struggled daily to maintain the power and money they had earned. He wondered if they thought it was worth it.

"Exactly. The thing is, I've been poor and I wouldn't mind being poor again. I'm not afraid of losing everything and that makes me very dangerous. I think it's time to flex the power I've spent the past years accumulating. But first, I want to see Marcus. Do you think you can help me sneak over to see him?"

Logan turned around as Bree got out of bed and slipped into her hospital gown. Having spent the evening with her, he had already learned that it would be useless to tell her she needed to rest. Instead, he enjoyed the flash of bottom she gave him as she tried to clasp the back of her gown closed. When had hospital gowns turned so sexy?

"You don't have to laugh," Bree said with a blush to her cheeks as she used one hand to steady herself on Logan and the other to hold her gown closed.

"I'm not laughing. I'm appreciating the view," Logan said in a rough voice as he slid his arm around her waist and led her from the room.

There was something about this woman that drew him

to her. She wasn't helpless by any means. He may have rescued her, but he had a feeling she was the one rescuing him.

The longer they walked, the more Bree leaned on him. He should have made her take a wheelchair to where Marcus was being monitored. He probably should have told her she was mooning the entire ICU and the security guards who were following at a discrete distance, but he was enjoying sneaking peeks of her cute, apple-shaped bottom.

Logan helped her into Marcus's room and sat her down on the chair. Tears streamed down her cheeks as she looked at her site manager lying in bed with one leg amputated below the knee. Logan squeezed her shoulder gently and bent down to whisper in her ear.

"There's a good chance he can hear you. You can fall apart as soon as I get you back into the hall, but for now you need to be strong for him."

Bree gave a silent nod of her head and took some deep breaths as she tried to control the emotions wreaking havoc on her. Her stomach had turned to knots and then plummeted the second she saw Marcus. His face was pale but no longer covered with a breathing tube. His knee was wrapped and he was sedated from the surgery.

Bree reached a shaky hand out to cover Marcus's. "Marcus, it's Bree. You saved me, Marcus. You have to wake up so I can kiss you and my mom can smother you with love. Plus there are some really cute nurses here who have totally been checking you out."

"What are you doing in here?" a nurse asked as she hurried into the room.

"He's a friend of mine. I was just thanking him for saving my life," Bree told her. She wasn't going to apologize for sneaking in. Instead she leaned forward and whispered into Marcus's ear. "Here's a nurse now. I bet if you show her your dimples she'll give you a sponge bath. I'll be back again to check on you. Thank you, Marcus. You'll always be my hero."

Bree placed her lips on his cheek and pulled back. With a silent nod to Logan, he hurried her from the room as the nurse checked on Marcus. Bree made it ten feet down the hall before she lost it. Logan stopped walking and pulled her to him. She felt her legs go out as she buried her head in his shoulder and cried. She knew Logan wouldn't let her fall. He didn't say a thing. He just held her as she cried for Marcus, cried for herself, and cried because she felt that was all she could do.

She didn't know how long Logan held her, but finally the tears stopped. The helpless feeling faded and a resolve unlike anything she'd ever felt filled her.

"Are you okay?"

"I am now. Thank you. Can I ask you a favor?"

"Anything."

"I need a computer." Bree stepped away from Logan's embrace. She wasn't going to be released until tomorrow. That gave her all night to work.

"For what?"

"Sometimes the only way to handle a bully is to fight back. I'm going to show him how much power I have and that I'm not afraid to use it."

Bree tried to send Logan home, but the stubborn man wouldn't leave. He'd fallen asleep hours ago in the chair beside her bed. How she could feel this close to someone she'd just met, she didn't know. But she did. And even more, she trusted him.

"Mom, you can go home now," Bree whispered.

Bree's family had gone to her favorite fast food place and brought her back a snack. Her mother had stayed while the others left. Her mother wore a pained look as she sat in an uncomfortable chair by the bed.

"I have to know you're safe, honey."

"I am. I have two huge men guarding the door."

Margret stood and began to pace as she looked back and forth between Bree, the security guards, and a sleeping Logan. "I'll leave if you promise to get some sleep."

Bree loved her mom. Sleep and chicken soup could cure anything. "Yes, Mom."

Margret planted a kiss on her cheek and headed for the door with a sigh. "I'll be back first thing in the morning."

Bree flipped through the television channels. There was too much going on in her head to sleep. She replayed the events of the day. She eyed the laptop Logan had brought along with a stuffed bulldog. Bree laughed at the ugly toy but kept it by her all night. She'd also seen Logan fight to keep his temper under control when she received flowers from both Trevor and Jeff.

Logan was turning out to be full of surprises. She reached over and pulled his laptop onto her bed and got to work. Bree pulled up the local news and smiled. On the front page was a picture of her asleep in the hospital bed with gauze wrapped around her head. She'd had Logan take it and she'd used an anonymous email that Drake set up for her to send it to the media along with "insider" details on the way the cops behaved and what really happened at the construction site.

She pulled up her own email and sent a note to both

Trevor and Jeff thanking them for the flowers and asking them for a meeting to "help her out with something." She knew they wouldn't be able to resist. By the time the sun was up, she had meetings set up for Monday. The next thing was a call to Mallory.

"Hey. Sorry to wake you so early. I need everything you have on Trevor Marion and Jeff Henderson. And I mean, everything—legal or not. Bank records, affairs, pictures, and anything else I can use."

"What are you going to do with it?" Mallory asked.

"Use it to figure out who's behind this and then destroy them," Bree said simply.

"Be careful, Bree. Voltaire knew what he was talking about when he said, 'With great power comes great responsibility.'"

"I am being responsible. I'm ridding the world of these leeches. These are people who would lie, cheat, steal, and murder innocent people."

"But if you lie, cheat, and steal to prove them wrong, aren't you just as bad?" Mallory asked. "I'll get you the information, but it will take some time. I know you, Bree. Don't let them win by turning you into one of them."

Chapter Eight

L ogan awoke to the sound of Bree on the phone. He rubbed his hands over his face and stretched his neck. So much for spending the night in the hospital to get rest. Bree finally hung up with someone named Noah and immediately started working on the laptop.

"Bree, have you been up all night?"

"Yes."

She was so focused on her work that he knew it would be like talking to a wall if he mentioned she needed to sleep. He'd never seen a look of such sheer determination before. The doctor came in to look her over before he could ask her what she was doing.

"You look good. I want you to go home and rest for a couple days. Call if you're having any headaches, blurry vision, or shooting light in your eyes. But, Miss Simpson," he said, closing the laptop, "you need to get off that computer and rest."

Bree smiled. "Yes, doctor."

Logan almost laughed. It was clear she was going to do no such thing.

"And no driving. Can your boyfriend take you home?"

Bree shot a glance at Logan, and he realized neither of them jumped to correct the doctor.

"Yes, I can. Are there any care instructions besides

tying her to the bed to make her rest?" Oh God, he shouldn't have said that. The images going through his mind certainly did not involve resting.

"The nurse will go over them when you check out," the doctor said before signing some papers and heading to the nurses' station to begin the check-out process.

"You don't have to take me home. I'm sure my mom will be here any minute. She's an early riser."

"It's okay. I don't mind taking care of you. I rather like it actually," Logan said with a slight upturn of his lips. He liked the way Bree blushed and wondered if there was anyone out there who did take care of her. She hadn't mentioned a boyfriend and certainly one would have turned up by now if she had one.

"Good morning, dear. How are you feeling? I heard the good news that you're able to go home. I have the car out front all ready to go." Margaret sailed into the room with a smile as bright as the sun.

"I'm feeling much better," Bree told her mother.

"Hmm. You're up to something. I can see it written all over your face. A mother knows these things." Margaret's smile disappeared into a thin line as she shook her finger at her daughter.

"Just getting some work done before I have to go home and rest."

Logan almost laughed. She was a horrible liar, and it was clear Margaret didn't believe it for a second. Instead of pushing, though, Margaret just shook her head. "I'll be here when you're ready to tell me. Now, let's get you dressed."

Logan stood up to leave as Margaret came over to him and gave him a motherly hug. "Thank you for staying with her, Logan. I felt so much better knowing she wasn't alone. You're a brave boy." She patted his arm and smiled up at him.

"Thank you, Mrs. Simpson."

"I'll take it from here. But I expect you at dinner the day after tomorrow at my house. Bree will call with all the details."

"Mom!" Bree's eyes widened and then rolled at her mother's matchmaking. It was clear she thought Logan was Bree's best bet for a boyfriend, and Margaret was going to bribe him with food to keep him around.

Logan's deep chuckle filled the room. "I'll leave her in your more-than-capable hands, Mrs. Simpson. And I look forward to dinner."

Logan turned to Bree and smiled at her. He wished he could kiss her, but their first kiss wouldn't be a quick kiss on the lips with her mom in the room. No, it would be full of roaming hands as lips met and tongues battled for power.

"I'll see you soon, Bree. Call me if you need anything."

"I would if I didn't need to go through your secretary," Bree grinned back at him.

Logan shot her a lopsided grin and wrote down his number. "Now you have no excuse not to call me. I'll talk to you soon." He gave her a wink and then sauntered out the door.

Logan spent the rest of the day at his hotel working the phone. He was calling every contractor, architect, and builder he knew to find out everything he could about Trevor Marion and Jeff Henderson. So far he'd learned that both Trevor and Jeff were old-school contractors fighting for every ounce of business, using every dirty-handed tactic they could. They paid off inspectors, donated heavily to political campaigns, and made sure to rub elbows with every investment manager.

Both were known to use intimidation as a means to get the highest paying jobs: photos of decision-makers' wives, tires slashed, windows broken with baseball bats, and so on. There had even been a couple stories of children coming home from school with messages for their daddies. The younger generation disapproved of these methods, but they were too afraid to stand up to the old-line power of Trevor and Jeff. Those who tried usually moved out of Georgia after their businesses collapsed. Typically, there had never been any direct evidence to link Trevor or Jeff. Until now, they were enjoying free rein to terrorize their competition.

Logan asked everyone he knew at Clarke Group about this "old friend" of his boss with no luck. No one knew who it was. Letting out a frustrated breath, Logan paced the room. He looked out at the construction site right in time to see a pink hard hat disappear into what was left of the corporate center.

"What the hell is she doing?" Logan cursed as he grabbed his room key and dashed out the door.

Bree had snuck out of her mother's house. She was pretty proud of it actually. At thirty-one, she was impressed she could still jump out her window into the large maple tree and climb down just like she used to when she was a teenager.

Her mother was babying her so much she felt smothered. She had always been a doer, and sitting in her old bed, staring up at her canopy, thinking of all the things that needed to be done, had gotten to her. The urge to get her hands dirty and fix as much as she could drove her to literally jump out the window.

She had sneaked into her closet and made some phone calls before jumping. The men were going to meet her at the construction site in a bit, but first she wanted to get a look at the damage and formulate a plan of action.

Bree had been so focused on assessing the outer structure that she didn't realize she had approached the site of the explosion. She and Marcus were lucky to be alive. She froze as she looked at the damage. In her mind, she wasn't seeing the downed beam or the fire damage. She was seeing them walking around, looking at the vandalism. The two imaginary figures walked past her and she shouted for them to watch out, but her memories didn't listen. The explosion sounded and she looked up to see the beam about to fall on her. The feel of Marcus's hands shoving her in the back was so real she stepped forward as she watched herself being pushed. The ceiling collapsed and everything went dark.

"Bree! Come back to me, sweetheart."

She blinked as the blackness receded and saw Logan's chest come into view. His arms were wrapped around her and he was talking her down from the horrible memory.

"It's not real, sweetheart. I'm real. I'm here and you're safe," he said softly as he stroked her back.

"I'm okay," Bree mumbled as she tried to stop looking at the beam. She'd somehow let it sneak up on her. It was the surprise of seeing the site for the first time that sent her mind hurtling back to the event.

"What are you doing here?" Logan asked with a little censure to his voice.

Bree pulled back from him and prepared for a fight. "I'm taking care of my business. I have families who depend on me, and I'm not going to be intimidated."

Logan shook his head and Bree was about to argue when she saw the way his lips quirked. "You're one badass lady, but I wouldn't expect anything less from someone who flew all the way to England to chew me out. What can I do to help?"

Bree let out a breath and smiled back to him. It felt good to have someone in her corner. "I need to assess what's good and what needs to go. I think the foundation is fine, but the internal structure is shot. I have three months until my first milestone. If I don't make it, then I lose the project."

Logan looked around and hid his reaction to her news. He'd do everything he could, but there wasn't much to be done except get the equipment in and start building again. However, he couldn't imagine hitting that timeline.

He watched as Bree walked around and took notes. She started talking to herself as she wrote in her notebook while Logan took a good look at what was left to work with. He could modify the plans to make the best use of what was still sound and save Bree some time and money.

"I have an idea . . ." Bree muttered before pulling out her phone and walking outside. Logan trailed after her and found the site filling with trucks.

Big Al recognized him and wrapped Logan in a bear hug, lifting him off the ground. "It's the guy who saved our Bree!"

Suddenly men who wanted to shake his hand and slap his back surrounded Logan.

"We never did find out your name," Al said with one large hand clasping Logan's shoulder.

"Logan Ward. And you?"

Al's smile slid from his face. Suddenly Big Al looked ready to pummel him as his hand tightened painfully on Logan's shoulder.

"You're the architect who's been screwing us over," Al growled as the other men closed in angrily around him. "We're going to miss our milestone and get laid off because of you."

"Gentlemen!" Bree clapped her hands and then rolled her eyes at herself. She'd just sounded like her mother. "Big Al, could you put Logan down, please?"

Al loosened his grip and Logan realized he'd been standing on his tiptoes as Al pulled him up off the ground. The men reluctantly stepped away from him, so Logan took the chance to move next to Bree. He was man enough to admit when he could be taken in a fight. Right now the only thing standing between him and a pissed-off crew was Bree.

"It's so good to see all of you. I can't thank you enough for what you did to save Marcus and me." Bree stepped forward and hugged the men. "I wouldn't be here without your quick thinking."

Logan watched in wonder as the men melted and blushed at Bree's praise. He'd never seen a crew like this. Most of the time, women in this industry were either secretaries or site managers' wives. But Bree somehow exuded both authority and camaraderie unlike anyone he'd ever seen before.

"We're just sorry we couldn't finish the project for you, Miss Bree," Big Al said as his shoulders slumped.

"That's why I called you here today. If we work like hell, we can meet the first milestone, then continue redoubled efforts to reach the second milestone early." Logan watched the look of confusion wash over her crew. "We were only days from reaching the first milestone, and the second is scheduled for three months from now. I intend to hit both in the next two months."

The crew erupted with questions and disbelief. Logan

had never seen a more passionate crew, but they would need twice as many men if they wanted to accomplish that.

Bree held up a hand and the group quieted down. "First, there are some things you need to know." Bree told them about the letters, about the possibility of Trevor or Jeff being behind the delays, and about how Logan hadn't been the problem at all. That earned him another bear hug from Big Al.

"I know many of you could find new jobs to hold you over. And I know many of your families depend on this job for a living. I am going to poach the best workers from Trevor and Jeff and it's going to piss them off something fierce. I'm going to use that bonus money to pay the extra workers. You'll have your same salary, but no bonus. After we get caught up, all bonuses will be split among the whole crew. Simpson Construction won't keep a dime of any further bonuses. What do you say?"

Big Al looked over the group and a big smile broke out across his leathered face. "I think the boys and I can help you with that. Let me make a list of men to contact."

Chapter Nine

Mallory was leaning against the old tree Bree had to climb to get back into her room at her mother's house. One perfectly red-heeled foot rested against the tree as she waited for Bree. In her hand, Bree saw two thick files and a deep frown marring Mallory's normally serene face.

"Aren't you supposed to be resting?"

"I had to meet with my crew and then the ATF. Damien managed to get them involved after Mom told him about Detective Gruber's gross incompetence. Do you have what I asked for?"

"Are you sure you want to do this? Once you go down this dark road, it may be hard to find your way back," Mallory warned.

"I've never been so sure about anything in my life. I've learned one thing about bullies: they won't stop until someone makes them."

"This isn't some schoolyard bully stealing your lunch money. These are ruthless men who will destroy innocent lives without blinking an eye."

"That's even more reason for me to do it," Bree said with determination. "Now, hand it over."

Mallory handed her the files. "Your family will never forgive me if something happens to you and I'll never forgive you if it does."

"Don't worry, Mal. I'm the middle child. If there's one thing I know how to do, it's to wreak havoc," Bree grinned before hoisting herself up into the tree.

Bree sat on the pink bedspread she'd had since she was a freshman in high school and opened the folder. She looked over Trevor's first. He was sixty-one years old. He was five feet seven inches tall. He was slowly balding with the hair on the sides of his head cut short and a graying mustache. Trevor's wife was considerably younger. Her name was Nikki and they had one child, a daughter. Nikki had a history of emergency room visits for "falls." Bree turned the page and pictures of Trevor with hookers took up a lot of the file. Some of the hookers were photographed the next day with bruises covering their faces.

She kept on turning page after page. Each one was worse than the others. Homes had been stolen out from under people and leveled for his construction projects. City bonds had been arranged that were now worthless. People had lost their savings investing in them while Trevor grew rich.

Bree looked at the financials. While Trevor was sleazy, she couldn't find any payments to government officials. She closed the folder and nibbled on her lower lip as she thought about all she had read. It didn't seem like it was Trevor. It was just a feeling she had. That meant it had to be Jeff. Bree hurriedly picked up Jeff's file and flipped it open to his picture. His light brown hair, dark tanned skin, and big, capped teeth suited the retirement homes in Florida more than running a major construction business.

Jeff was well built but had never dirtied his flawless hands during his fifty-nine years in the industry. Bree had spent summers in high school and college working on houses for charity and knew what it took to actually build something. She doubted Jeff did anything with his hands besides getting a manicure.

Turning the page, she read about his family connections to New York and Chicago. She read about the government contracts he received in Georgia when it was clear he never should have been awarded them. She saw reports of vandalism, threats, and hospital records from private owners like her who had thought about using someone else to construct their corporate buildings. Bree felt her heart race as she flipped to the back of the file to look over his financials. It had to be Jeff.

She skimmed the numbers and saw payments to super PACs and politicians' re-election campaigns, but nothing to the detective and police officer who had given her a hard time. Bree slammed the folder closed. Dammit! She had to find a link or no one would believe her.

The next afternoon, Logan stood in the lobby of Simpson Global and argued with the security guard. He didn't have a badge. He wasn't on the list. Bree wasn't in the office today. No matter what argument Logan put forward, the guard wasn't going to let him upstairs.

"Please, I just want to meet with Bree's assistant."

"You're not on the list and the office is about to close," the guard said again as he reached for his radio. Logan was sure he was going to be tossed out soon.

"George, it's okay. This young man is with me. I can vouch for him." Logan turned to his rescuer and choked on his thank-you.

Warning: Cougar on the Prowl was on the front of Shirley's walker as she shuffled over to where he and the security guard had been talking. George gave Shirley a smile and then went back to guarding the elevators at Simpson Global.

"Thank you, Shirley. I was just trying to find out where Bree lives. She's not answering her phone, and I thought it might be nice to take her some flowers," Logan said a little lamely.

It had sounded like a great idea when he passed the florist, but now he felt out of place with the huge bouquet in his hands. He'd also started to doubt if he should be taking someone flowers. It had been way too long since he'd been in a relationship, years in fact—since Stacy cheated on him, sending him to England. It wasn't easy facing your younger brother who was now married to your ex-fiancée with two perfect little boys toddling around. But Bree seemed different. She wasn't a woman you see for a short time and then forget. She was a woman you found yourself doing anything for—like taking her an obscenely large bouquet of flowers.

"Of course, dear. Tell me, who are your people?"

Uh-oh. That was a Southern interrogation technique. "I'm from Charleston, South Carolina. My family is proud to be one of the first families to settle there from England."

"You're a good Southern boy, are ya?"

"Yes, ma'am."

"Then why are you in England?" Shirley asked with a knowing eye. Somehow she already knew the story, or at least that there was one.

Logan pasted on a fake smile to hide the fact he was uncomfortable, but by the way Shirley raised one eyebrow he knew she saw through it. "My family, the Wards, is one of the most preeminent families in Charleston. We were brick builders from England and set up shop in Charleston before the American Revolution."

"I figured that was y'all. Simpson Construction buys bricks from your family."

"If you say so," Logan shrugged.

Shirley narrowed her eyes. "Are you not good with your family? Family is important, you know?"

"I know. It's my family who doesn't know that." Logan took a deep breath. Why was he telling this to an old lady who was probably going to tell everyone else? But one look at her and Logan knew he had to tell his story, or he wasn't getting Bree's address. "I met a girl in college and we became engaged. I didn't go home much because my father kept pressing me to join the family business."

"And you wanted to design, not build," Shirley guessed.

"That's right. Whenever I came home, it ended in an argument. My mother would come to me later and try to smooth things over. She was a peacemaker but never stood up for me when I needed it. She never questioned my father and it made me angry so I stayed away.

"Then I brought my fiancée home. Dinner went just as I figured it would. My father pressured me to join the company, and I told him I wanted to get my master's in architecture. My father exploded. He disowned me and gave the VP position to my younger brother, Brad. He also announced Brad would receive my half of the company and the inheritance he had always held over my head."

"So, you forged ahead on your own. And Stacy?" Shirley asked with no pity in her voice. Somehow that made Logan feel better. It also made him realize he had stopped pitying himself as well.

"I stormed out of the house in anger. I expected Stacy to follow. She didn't. Instead I found her in Brad's bed soon after. Two months later, she was pregnant and they became engaged. The next day, I left for England on scholarship. My father was true to his word and cut me off. In the only act of defiance my mother ever made, she sent me enough cash for the plane ticket and living expenses for one month."

"Have you seen them since?"

"When I have to. Brad and Stacy are married with two children and happily spending the family money. They enjoy rubbing it in my face every time I show up."

"Humph. That usually means the opposite is true. But it makes me like you more. If you were a prick like your brother, then I wouldn't let you near my Bree. But the question I still have is, what are your intentions with Bree? I will say you're definitely the cutest thing that's been hanging around here lately." Shirley winked.

"Wait, what do you mean, lately?" Logan didn't like the idea of other guys begging George to let them up to Bree's office.

"That's right. Bree is surrounded by men, but it will take a special man to get her attention. The question is, are you the one or are you just trying to have some fun before heading back across the pond?"

Logan was about to answer automatically that he was the right man, but Shirley had a point. What was he going to do? It wouldn't be fair to either of them to toy with emotions and then leave.

"I don't know," he said sadly. The thought of giving up on Bree so soon after meeting her filled him with despair. Could he turn his back on something that felt so right just because it was new? All he knew was when he thought about his future, he saw Bree in it. That had to mean something. "But, I intend to find out. That is, if I can get her address."

Shirley pulled out a piece of paper from the basket on her walker. Without saying a word, she wrote something down, folded it up, and tossed the paper on the floor. "Whoopsie—it slipped. Could you pick that up for me, dear?"

Logan shook his head and bent over to pick up the piece of paper. When he straightened back up and turned around, Shirley gave him a wink and scooted off to the elevators whistling. He opened the paper and saw an address and a message: *Take care of my girl or you'll answer to me.*

Later that night, Logan pulled up to the address Shirley had given him with a to-go container of chicken noodle soup and the flowers. He cut the engine and was trying to wrangle the flowers out of the car when he saw a dark shadow dart from behind the house. The figure ran down the block and disappeared.

Logan pushed the flowers back into the seat and ran around the car. He knew the sway of those hips even in the dark. What in the world was Bree up to? Turning his car around, he took off in the direction she had run. When he reached the end of the street, he saw the taillights of a cab as it took off. He didn't know what she was up to, but somehow he knew it wasn't a good idea.

The cab stopped and Bree got out. Logan parked his car and tried to catch up, but it was too late. She was gone.

Bree put on the ski mask as she approached Jeff's

construction site. She pulled out the wire cutters and looked around to see if anyone was coming. Clipping just enough wire to pull back the fence, she slid through the opening and headed to the trailer. Unlike all the damage Jeff had probably done to her site, she wasn't going to vandalize anything. No, she was after something far more damaging to Jeff . . . his employment records.

She snuck around a backhoe and plastered herself to the side of the trailer. Sliding through the shadows, she rounded the back and looked up at the window. Trailers got so hot in the summer, the window was usually open with a fan in it. AC units could only do so much and she had a feeling Jeff was the type not to install them unless he had to. Sure enough, a box fan sat in the open window.

Bree looked around until she found a piece of lumber. Leaning it against the side of the trailer, she crawled up to the open window. She reached inside and set the box fan down. After climbing through the window, she landed on the table underneath and moved over to the filing cabinet.

Her heart was surprisingly calm as she opened the drawer and pulled out the latest payroll statement. She took out her phone and snapped a picture. She slid the file back in place and closed the cabinet. Through the open window, she heard footsteps approaching the trailer. Looking around frantically, she tried to hide before the front door was thrown open. She felt a little silly having gone through all the trouble of climbing through the window only to discover the front door was unlocked. But the humor was lost under the pounding of her heart as she tried to make herself invisible.

"Bree?" The deep voice asked in a harsh whisper.

Bree popped her head out from behind the fern on top of the filing cabinet and stared down at Logan.

"What are you doing here?"

"I think the better question is, how did you get up there?" Logan put his hands on his hips and shook his head at her.

"I'm the reigning champion of the Simpson Family Hide and Seek Tournament. I'll never give away my secrets," she said, realizing she felt better just having him here with her.

Logan held up his arms in silent invitation as he laughed. Bree smiled in response and slid forward. Logan's hands wrapped around her waist and Bree put her hands on his wide shoulders. When he lifted her down, her breasts brushed against him. Logan lowered her slowly, making sure she slid down the whole length of his hard body. Bree felt the excitement from the break-in mix with the sexual tension that had started the second he saved her.

"You do realize what you're doing is illegal, right?" Logan asked, lowering his voice.

Bree shot him a smirk. "Only if you get caught." She tried to pull away, but Logan kept his hands around her waist. She felt his fingers flex and saw raw hunger in his eyes.

"What are you doing here, Bree?" he asked again, his voice turning seductive as his hands moved to her hips.

"You'll never get it out of me," Bree said with more bravado than she felt. Especially when she realized she'd been leaning into him. *Way to stay in control,* her mind chided.

Logan's fingertips danced along her back as he pulled her against him. "I can think of a way, many ways in fact, to get it out of you. I'll warn you, it may take all night."

Bree suddenly felt out of breath. Men usually did one of two things. They were such pushovers they did whatever she said or they tried to overpower her and take complete control of her. Logan was different.

And therein lay the difference between him and other men who had tried to be completely alpha. Logan was secure enough with himself that he didn't have to try. He just was. And that is what made Bree long for him to do exactly what he threatened to do.

"Really?" she tried to say as calmly as she could while feeling Logan's hand skimming her rib cage.

"Really. It's just too bad someone's coming or I'd show you," he whispered against her ear.

"What?" Bree said loudly before Logan's hand clamped over her mouth.

"Smooth, Simpson. I just heard a truck pull up. We need to get out of here."

"We can go out the way I got in." Bree hurried to the table and pushed Logan toward it. "You first. I can move quicker and hide if need be."

"I don't like . . ."

"Oh, I know. You're the big, bad man and you want to protect me. But in this case, it's better for you to go first."

Reluctantly, Logan climbed onto the table as the sound of truck doors closing reached them. It took some angling, but he made it out the window. Bree threw her leg out the window and slid the rest of her body through before turning around and placing the fan back in front of the open window.

"Come on," Logan whispered.

"Wait a minute," Bree whispered back. She had to see who it was.

The door opened and two security guards flashed their lights around the trailer. Bree ducked and listened to the men complaining about their girlfriends and having to watch chick flicks. Disappointed not to find any more clues, Bree let Logan pluck her from the ramp she had made. Quietly, she helped him pick up the board and put it back in place before ducking under the fence.

Chapter Ten

L ogan parked the car a block away and walked around to open Bree's door. The ski mask hung in her hand as she got out. The ride to her mother's house had been quiet. They both had felt the crazy energy in the trailer and neither knew quite what to say about it.

"Over here. Mrs. King goes to bed early and won't see us sneaking across her backyard," Bree said as she reached for his hand.

Logan laced his fingers with hers and used his thumb to trace her palm slowly. The tension slammed into him as he felt her shiver in response. "You know you could just use the front door."

"And let my mother know I was gone? I'd never hear the end of it," she laughed.

The sweet sound had an instant reaction on him. As they stopped beside a large tree in her backyard, he wished nothing more than to grab her and race back to his hotel and make love to her all night. But what would Shirley say? He had some major decisions to make before he could be with Bree.

"Um," Bree started in a hushed voice, "thanks for looking out for me tonight."

Logan looked down at her upturned face and when she nervously ran her tongue over her bottom lip, he decided he'd let Shirley kill him, because what a way to go! He bent down and captured her lips. He didn't start slowly. He didn't ask permission like a gentleman should. No, he invaded. His fingers speared her hair as he thrust his tongue into her mouth, knowing Bree would either bite him or give as good as she got.

He had his answer when she ground against him and moaned. Logan backed her up against the large tree and used it to shield them from view. Bree was already pulling his dress shirt from his jeans as he shoved her shirt and bra up to expose her breasts. Bree bit his lower lip and Logan wanted to strip her naked right then and there. Instead he bent his head and scraped his teeth along her raised nipple before sucking it fully into his mouth.

Bree grabbed his head and held him to her as he cupped her other breast. He squeezed and she closed her eyes, enjoying his hands on her. "Bree, I don't want to stop."

"Then don't," she panted as she tried to pull him to her again.

Logan captured her lips again as his fingers worked her into a frenzy. He pushed against her and she inhaled sharply when his erection rubbed against her. Tearing his lips away and taking a step back, Logan stood breathing heavily.

"Damn, Bree," he whispered in reverence.

Bree slumped against the tree and took a deep breath. She shivered as the air blew on her bare breasts. She just nodded at Logan.

"I take it you kinda like me then, huh?" Logan grinned. He'd never been so lost in someone before. It was as if they consumed each other.

"It's probably just the head wound," Bree joked as

Logan reached forward and pulled down her bra with a sigh.

"Probably. But if that's what it takes for a guy like me to get a woman like you, then I'll take it." Logan paused and looked at her. "I don't want to be a one-night stand. I want more of you than that. I want to wake up beside you. I want to spoil you, take you on dates, show you what you're beginning to mean to me. You deserve that."

"Logan, what about when you leave?" Bree swallowed hard. She was a strong woman, and he could tell she wasn't going to cry at the thought of a guy leaving her.

"I don't know. It's why I don't want to rush. If I slept with you, then it would kill me to leave you. I couldn't bear to think I hurt you."

Bree stepped forward and placed her head on his chest, listening to his strong heartbeat. Logan cupped the back of her head with one hand and the other ran up and down her back as he held her. They stood there holding each other for a long time.

"You better get inside. I'll see you tomorrow for dinner."

"Dinner?"

"Yeah, remember? Your mom invited me."

Bree groaned. "Oh God. Our first date is going to be dinner with my family."

"It'll be our second. We did a little breaking and entering for our first date. I even got a kiss goodnight."

Bree rolled her eyes and had to smother a laugh. She reached up and grabbed the low-hanging branch. She leaned forward and brushed a kiss on his cheek. "Best first date ever," she whispered in his ear before pulling herself up into the tree.

Logan watched until she climbed into her window and gave her one last wave before heading around the house.

"Yoo-hoo! Mr. Ward!" Logan whipped around at the sound of the woman hailing him. Margaret Simpson stood at the open front door with a tray in her hands and a dishtowel thrown over her shoulder. "Thank you for making sure Bree got home safely tonight. We'll see you tomorrow for dinner?"

Logan shot a glance to the back of the house and Margaret just smiled serenely. "I've known about the tree since she was sixteen and used it for the first time to sneak out. Just don't tell her I know," Margaret winked and held out her tray. "Cookie?"

Logan plastered a smile on his face. His hair was messed up and he was pretty sure his shirt was only partly buttoned. "No, thank you, Mrs. Simpson. I look forward to seeing you tomorrow night, though."

"Good. I look forward to getting to know you better. Obviously my daughter already has. Good night, Mr. Ward." Margaret sent him one last smile and then closed the door with her hip.

Finally looking down at himself, Logan saw he had managed only three buttons. He groaned when he saw his reflection in his car window and silently cursed. His lips were swollen from kissing. His dark hair was a mess and there were nail marks across part of his exposed chest. Dinner tomorrow was going to be hell. What did he take to the hostess to say *thanks for inviting me even though I almost had sex with your daughter against your tree*?

Bree sat in her office and looked over the folders Mallory had given her the night before. Trevor was due in that morning and then Jeff would meet with her in the afternoon. One way or the other, she was going to get to the bottom of this.

Noah buzzed her and she pressed her intercom button. "Mr. Marion is here to see you."

"Let him wait ten minutes and then show him in. Let it slip I'm on a call with the owners of the corporate center."

"Yes, ma'am. Sorry to interrupt your call with the owners. I hope everything is okay with the corporate center."

Bree made a note to give Noah a raise at his next review before picking up the phone. She dialed the first number Big Al had given her. "Hi, Todd. This is Bree Simpson of Simpson Steel and Construction. Al gave me your number and said you'd make a great site manager." Bree nodded as Todd talked even though no one could see her doing it. Then she smiled. "Yes, I know you're Jeff Henderson's site manager, but I'm prepared to pay you more than Jeff ever would. I appreciate my workers' opinions and my workers say you're the best. I want you to join my team."

Bree threw out a number and put a check mark next to Todd's name after he eagerly agreed to meet with her tomorrow. One down and a whole crew to go.

"Miss Simpson, Mr. Marion is here to see you," Noah said formally as he showed Trevor into her office.

Trevor's beady eyes reminded Bree of a rat. He eyed the office as if it were his and ignored her until he had surveyed the entire room. He slowly made his way to the chair in front of Bree's desk and lowered himself into it. It was only after he crossed his legs that he looked up and met her eyes.

"I won't tell you 'I told you so,' but I hear you're not going to make your first milestone." Trevor didn't bother to hide his glee. "It was always too big of a job for a little lady like you. I'll be happy to step in and save the project for you. Just have all the files sent to my office."

Bree sat and waited as Trevor talked. He was so arrogant it never occurred to him that Bree would have him here for any other reason but to hand over the project. So, she waited. She listened to the comments she'd been hearing since shop class—a woman didn't know construction, a woman couldn't run a company as large as Simpson Steel and Construction, a woman couldn't work with all those men and remain a lady . . . wink, wink. Bree managed to remain impassive until Trevor finally talked himself out.

"Thank you for your generous offer of assistance, Trevor, but that's not why I called you here," Bree said with a bored look on her face.

"It's not? Don't you know . . ."

Bree held up her hand and just shook her head. "It's my turn to talk now. I have every intention of hitting my milestone. The reason I asked you here was to find out if you had a hand in the explosion at my site."

Trevor's eyes went wide and he began to sputter. "How dare you!" he finally roared. "Why would you think I would even concern myself with your project, much less actually try to interfere with it?"

"Simple—money. You need it for all the bribes you're paying out." Bree slid a picture of his former secretary across to him. Both eyes were black and there were clear fingermarks around her neck. "I believe this one cost you a $600,000 house in Florida and $2,000,000 in cash. She's just one of many, as you know."

"You bitch!" Trevor's face turned a dangerous shade of red as he leapt up from his chair.

Bree just smiled. "Why, yes, I am. I'm glad you finally realize that. Now sit down and shut up."

She could see Trevor debating, but he sat down anyway. "You want money now, too? All you whores stick together."

"I want to know everything you know about the vandalism and the explosion at my site. And don't tell me you don't know anything."

Trevor fell back against the chair and stared at her. A trickle of sweat ran down the side of his face. With a long exhale he sat forward. "All I know is you've pissed someone off. The talk on the street is he will pay anyone who disrupts your build."

"How could he do that and remain unknown?" Bree asked.

"It's all done online now. He has the vandal take a picture of himself with the mischief they caused and send it to him electronically. Once verified, he sends cash in the mail. He's smart enough to cover his tracks, too. Then he retains the picture of the vandal for blackmail if they ever talk. I've only heard whispers of it and haven't been able to learn more. No one is talking because they don't want the money to dry up."

"See, that wasn't so hard, was it?" Bree said sweetly.

"What are you going to do with that photo?" Trevor asked nervously.

Bree smiled again and tucked it into her drawer. "I think I'll just hold onto this. If I hear of you touching another woman," Bree paused for effect, "I will ruin you. And I'll enjoy it. Goodbye, Trevor."

Bree dismissed him and looked down at the file in front

of her. Her heart was pounding, and she couldn't read a single word on the page, but it held her interest as Trevor steamed. Finally he gave up and stormed from the office. She didn't breathe until the door slammed behind him.

"Do you believe him?" Mallory's soft voice asked as she stepped out of Bree's bathroom.

"I think so. After looking at the reports you gave me, I think Jeff's behind it. Trevor is all brute and no brains. At first glance, the things that happened to the project and me appear to be brute force. But really it's far more complicated. Just enough destruction to delay the project and get me fired. The ATF said that the explosion wasn't so much to destroy the whole build as to just damage it a little."

Mallory sat in the chair Trevor had just occupied and crossed her legs. Red stilettos bounced as she thought. "I'm going to withhold judgment until I see Jeff. What are you going to do with those pictures?"

Bree grinned and pulled out a file. "I've already made copies and they're ready to be sent to the local and state police. And maybe one or two news stations. I want to wait until this whole matter is settled and then Trevor will pay for his crimes. Hopefully, my threat of blackmail will keep him in line until then."

"I won't say it again, but you're playing a dirty game here. You need to be prepared for the mud that will be flung. It goes both ways, you know. I can almost guarantee Trevor is having someone turn over every rock, roommate, and boyfriend you've ever had to find dirt on you. After all, it's what I would do."

"I know. I'm ready for it."

Bree's cocky attitude slipped a little as she waited for Jeff Henderson to walk into her office. When it came to power players in Atlanta, Jeff was at the top. He had successfully kept his position at the top by ruthlessly squashing competition. That led her to believe he was the man behind her attempted ouster. And it made her worry at the same time.

She knew it was both a fault and an asset that she tended to be cavalier. When dealing with the big boys of Atlanta, a woman could not be afraid to take risks. But now she was playing with her father's legacy as well. If Jeff took her down, then he would take Simpson Steel with her.

"Mr. Henderson to see you, Miss Simpson." Noah stepped aside as Jeff sauntered in.

Unlike Trevor, Jeff entered the room and his gaze never left hers. His dark hair was sprinkled with a dash of silver and swooped over his broad forehead. His dark brown suit fit his thick but solid shape to perfection. It was also more expensive than most of Bree's own clothes. His shined shoes didn't have a scuff on them. Jeff was making a statement.

Bree felt her stomach flip. Her palms grew sweaty. Jeff literally wore his power, and it was hard not to be intimidated by it. Bree kept a pleasant smile on her face, but refused to stand when Jeff stopped right in front of her desk and held out his hand.

"Thank you so much for coming all the way down here to see me, Jeff." Bree poured on her best Southern belle as she shook his hand.

"Anything for you, darlin'. It's not every day a pretty lady asks me to come see her," Jeff said with a wink, still holding her hand.

Bree smiled graciously. This whole scene was going to be played out on the battlefield known as good Southern graces. The sweeter the compliment, the sharper the dagger.

"Aren't you just the kindest thing? You'll give a girl a big head with compliments like those."

"You should hear them every day. If I was lucky enough to wake up beside you every morning, you'd dine on compliments for breakfast." Jeff traced his thumb over her knuckles and Bree tried not to gag.

Instead she giggled and felt brain cells dying as she did so. "Oh, Jeff!" She pulled her hand out of his and flirtingly smacked him with it.

Jeff finally sat down and crossed his legs. He rested his laced fingers on his knee and took on a look of concern. "It's so horrible what happened to you. Are you sure you should be working so soon after the accident? You're such a delicate rose, I'd hate to see you lose your bloom."

Bree put her hand to her chest and gave him a soft smile. "Thank you for your concern. But as you know, roses have thorns and are not as delicate as they appear." Bree let the challenge sink in as she leaned forward conspiratorially. "Actually, Jeff, that's why I called you. I knew if anyone could help me, it would be you."

"Of course. What can Jeff do for you?"

"I was hoping you could tell me if you blew up my building." Jeff's saccharine smile froze on his face as Bree smiled politely back at him. "I'd sure hate to think you did."

Jeff pushed his smile back into place. "Darlin', why would you ever think I'd do something like that?"

Bree sighed and shook her head slowly. "Really, it hurts my heart to even say anything, but—" Bree pulled out her file and spread out pictures of Jeff at political rallies with the mayor, "—you're the only one with enough power to buy the police, and we both know Trevor Marion is too dumb to pull off the sabotage of my build. He lacks your wonderful sense of finesse."

"I'm afraid you need to go back home and rest, darlin'. Let us men handle these things for you. It was an unfortunate accident, but an accident is what it was. Don't be ruining folks' good names just because you lost control of your build."

Jeff stood up and looked down at her sadly. "I expect this is the end of these silly accusations. Regardless of this minor lapse in judgment, I want you to know you don't need to worry your pretty little head about the build. I've already talked to the owners and will be taking over the build in three months when you don't make your milestone. I just want you to know I'm proud of you, and I'm sure your daddy, God rest his soul, would be, too, for attempting a project this size. You have nothing to be embarrassed about."

Bree dug her high heel into the plush carpet, imagining she was squashing Jeff. "That's kind of you to say, Jeff. Thank you for easing my mind."

Jeff smiled at her patronizingly. "Anytime, darlin'. Now, I have another appointment. I need to finish another build before starting on the corporate center. Go home and rest, darlin'. Jeff's here to take care of everything."

Bree waited until he was at her door before stopping him. "Oh dear, are you talking about your build outside of town?"

"Yes?"

"I'm so sorry. I think I might have done something wrong." Bree's face showed worry while hiding the glee. "See, since the explosion almost cost the life of my site manager, I had to get a new one. Some of my crew recommended Todd. And well, he agreed." Bree cringed dramatically. "Not only that, but it appears Todd's really well liked and half of the crew he was working with is coming with him to help me reach my milestone."

Jeff's smile fell from his face. "You poached my crew?"

Bree's eyes went wide. "I guess I did. Was that wrong?"

Jeff's eyes turned black. The coldness behind them scared the crap out of Bree. "Don't worry, darlin', I'll find a way to make it even."

Jeff turned and walked out the door with the threat hanging in the air. Bree let out a shaky breath. It was all fun and games until that point. Jeff didn't mind taking her business from her, and she knew she'd just thrown down the gauntlet by disrupting his.

Mallory quietly stepped from the bathroom and took a seat in front of Bree's desk. "I'll give it to you, you have tits of steel to stand up to him."

"What do you think?" Bree asked.

"I think you'd better watch out. You've pissed off two men today who have even more reason to see you run out of town. What are you going to do now?"

Bree looked at her watch and let her head fall forward to gently bang on her desk. "I have to go to my mom's for dinner. She invited Logan."

"What's wrong with that?"

"I almost had sex with him against a tree last night," Bree groaned.

"Now we're talking!"

Bree's head shot up as she and Mallory's eyes went wide. Thirty seconds later, Shirley rolled into the office.

"Don't stop. I want to hear more."

Mallory shrugged. "Hey, I'm single now, I want to hear more, too."

Bree groaned again and went back to banging her head on the desk. "I like him," she whined.

"Hot damn!" Shirley reached over and high-fived Mallory.

Bree kept banging her head. "But he's from London! And he's cocky, but in a cute way. And he saved my life and never left my side . . . maybe it's just hero worship. Right?"

"You don't get frisky against a tree to say thanks for saving my life. You get frisky against a tree because you can't keep your hands off of each other."

"Good point, Shirley," Mallory grinned. "I like him. Go for it. The worst that will happen is you have really hot sex and then he leaves, but at least you'll get the really hot sex."

"For as tough as I am, I don't like to have hot sex and then never see the guy again. I'm actually old-fashioned. And I'm afraid I'm already getting too attached. I refuse to be that clingy girlfriend who demands he stays here." Bree lifted her head and looked at her two friends. "I have to pull back or I'll be a blubbery mess when he goes home in two weeks."

Shirley snorted and Mallory shook her head. "You should pull something, but 'back' is not it," Bree felt her face turn red as she stared in shock at Shirley.

"Shirley!"

"What? I'm too old to beat around the bush. Listen to me. That boy is a keeper. Plus he has a really nice butt." Shirley turned to Mallory to explain. "When he bent over to pick up a piece of paper for me—"

"Enough!" Bree wanted to stick her fingers in her ears and sing la-la-la.

"You know you're like a little sister to me. So I say this with all the love I have for you: this guy pushes you while supporting you, and I think you need to give him a chance."

With a *humph* in agreement, Shirley stood and left with Mallory. Bree stared out her window. She could still feel his hands on her and knew she wanted more. Never had she lost her head over someone so fast before. Never had she both dreamed of and feared the future before. She wanted more time with him, but that time was limited. However, when Logan kissed her, touched her, all she cared about was the now, and right now, all she cared about was seeing Logan again.

Chapter Eleven

L ogan pulled his rental car to a stop along the street outside of Margaret's house. He grabbed the bottles of wine and took some deep breaths. He had met Bree's family before, but this was different. This time her mom knew he . . . well, he *liked* her daughter. That, combined with the fact he hadn't met a girl's family since he was engaged, meant he had no clue what to do.

A knock on his window made Logan jump in his seat. Shirley's face peered in at him. "You're not going to chicken out, are you?" he heard her ask through the window.

"Of course not," Logan said as he opened the door.

Shirley just chuckled. "This will be fun."

"You get some sort of sick pleasure out of watching me squirm, don't you?"

"Since my soaps got cancelled, this is the most entertaining thing I've seen. And if it matters, I'm rooting for you." Shirley paused at the stairs leading up to the house. "Hang onto your pecker; here we go!"

Logan looked up right in time to see Margaret open the front door. "Shirley, Logan, so glad you both could join us tonight."

Logan smiled and handed her the wine. "Thank you for opening your house to me."

Margaret smiled back and Logan stepped into the

house. "That's not all that was apparently opened for him," she muttered quietly to Shirley.

Taken by surprise, Logan tripped on a rug and stumbled forward right toward Allegra's back. He reached out to stop his fall and found his hands wrapped around Allegra, where his hands couldn't help but grab onto her breasts. The force of his fall was too much for Allegra as she lost balance on her heels and teetered precariously before falling face first against Reid's side. Reid's bourbon went flying and landed on Drake as the three of them landed in a heap at Bree's feet.

"I wonder if there is a daughter of mine he hasn't felt up yet? Drake better watch out for Elle," Margaret murmured as she hurried to grab some club soda for Drake.

Logan groaned in embarrassment and wanted to hide his face. Except his face was inches from Allegra's lady parts and Bree was standing there tapping a foot with her arms crossed. Pulling his hands from Allegra's breasts, he sat up on his knees.

"I'm so sorry, Allegra."

Allegra smiled and reached up to grab Elle's hand. "That's okay. It was definitely the most memorable hello I've had."

When Logan looked up Bree's shapely leg to her face, he found she wasn't mad at all. A huge grin stretched ear to ear. Her shoulders shook with unvoiced laughter as she looked down on him.

Reid and Logan stood up and dusted off their pants. Grudgingly, Reid held out his hand. "I saw the video. I guess I should thank you."

"Reid!" Bree smacked her brother's arm.

"Fine. I should also say I was wrong about you. First impressions and all that."

Logan shook his hand. "I know all about first impressions not being right. But thank you. I'm happy to meet you all under much better circumstances."

Margaret hurried back into the room, took Drake's sports coat from him, and started washing it off. "Mallory just called. She's stuck at work and can't make it for dinner. But, she gave me some news."

"Is it about the notes I had dropped off at her office?" Reid asked.

Logan still hadn't seen them, but Bree had told him about them.

"Yes. Despite breaking up with Agent Wallace, they're still friends. He ran the notes through his lab off record — but nothing. No fingerprints and the envelopes and stamps were attached with adhesive, so no DNA either."

"Another one bites the dust," Allegra said sadly. "What went wrong? Damien was dreamy."

Elle just shrugged. "Who knows? But I'm not surprised. You know all of her relationships are short-lived."

Bree's shoulders sagged and Logan wrapped his arm around her. "I thought there would be something on those letters," she said.

Margaret handed Drake his coat. "It's okay. We'll find out who's behind this. The important thing is that you're okay."

Bree nodded. "I am. And I saw Marcus this morning. I only got to speak to him for a short time before the doctors shooed me out. After I stopped hugging him and thanking him for saving me, I told him Simpson Global was covering all his costs and also paying for a state-of-the-art prosthetic."

Elle nodded her head. "Good. I wanted to do that as well. And we'll help him with anything else he needs. He will always have a job with us if he wants it."

"Well, there's a spot of good news. I'll make him up a nice basket and take it to him tomorrow. The poor man lost a leg saving my daughter. The least I can do is make sure he has home-cooked food for every meal."

Bree squeezed Logan's hand and smiled at him. He was glad she had stopped thanking him. Logan wanted her to like him for who he was, not one thing he did.

Talk turned to wedding plans as Drake, Reid, and Logan slowly separated themselves to head out back for guy talk. Logan was glad they started treating him as one of the guys. Maybe Bree's whole family didn't hate him completely.

"So, what's the deal with you and Bree?"

Crap. Her brother wasn't going to let it go.

"As the new guy in the family, I feel I need to stick up for him. Go easy, Reid."

Logan smiled with relief. He had an ally. "Thanks, Drake."

"Don't thank me yet. Also as a member of the family, I have to give you a hard time because you're trying to become involved with my sister. Therefore, I'll just ask a little nicer than Reid. How are things going between you and Bree?"

"Seriously?" Logan looked between them. Hard eyes looked back at him. Yep, they were serious. "I like her and we're trying to get to know each other."

Reid and Drake stared at him some more. Finally they gave Logan a little nod of approval. "Just no more seeing my sister naked. I don't think I can handle that."

"How did you know about that?" Logan asked, surprised. Did everyone know what happened last night?

"I was there, remember?" After a short pause, it

dawned on Reid. "Oh damn, you're thinking of another time besides the hospital." Reid put his hands to his ears. "Don't tell me. You two better be getting married."

Drake broke out laughing and Logan just stood there. At times like these, he figured it was better to keep his mouth shut than to dig a deeper hole.

"Boys! Dinner's ready," Margaret called from the patio door before disappearing back inside.

Logan didn't know how, but it seemed an uneasy truce had been established. All through dinner, he fielded questions about his job, life in England, and his travels. By the end of dinner, he felt exhausted from the politest inquisition he'd ever had. But it was worth it when Margaret sent him a friendly smile before the discussion turned to Allegra's upcoming Fashion Week and the resort Elle, Drake, and Reid were working on.

Reid looked to Logan and could see an idea flash across his face. "I wanted to build a small concert hall for intimate performances, sporting events, and so on. I haven't found an architect I like yet. Too bad you're in England. I'd really like a designer on it who understands how to match it to the Southern elegance of the resort."

"I could do that. I can drive out and see it and then work up the plans in England. Unfortunately, I would have to get permission to do such a small project."

Reid shook his head. "It wouldn't matter. I'm touting this as the epitome of Southern luxury. I need a local on it. No matter that you're from this area; your office is in England and that wouldn't look right."

"I understand," Logan nodded. He'd been hired for the simple reason he was from a London firm numerous times. Clients thought it was exotic. "It's too bad, though. I've wanted to take up some projects like that. I love the big builds, but there's not much freedom in them when there are twenty owners, each having to have something he wants in it."

Margaret picked up the dessert plates as they started talking more about projects Logan wanted to do. He'd been feeling restless the past couple of years and talking about the ideas filled him with excitement. But soon the crowd broke up. Shirley headed home, and Elle and Drake hurried out soon after with sly smiles on their faces as they raced to the car.

"Thanks for taking care of me, Mom. I'm just going to grab something from my room and then head home," Bree told Margaret as she gave her a hug.

"Home? You *are* home."

"Mom, I'm fine. I want to get back to my place tonight. It's easier for me to get to the office in the morning."

"How are you even going to get there? Your car is still in the shop," Margaret worried.

"I'll drive her home. It can't be far from my hotel," Logan offered and tried not to let the excitement show in his voice.

Reid came over and dropped a kiss on his mom's head. "I won't say 'don't worry' because I know you will. I'll pick her up in the morning and take her to work. She can borrow one of my cars after the doctor has given her the all-clear to drive."

Margaret gave a sigh, but then kissed Bree's cheek. "I love you."

"I love you, too, Mom."

Bree ran upstairs and was back a minute later with her purse. Logan offered her his arm and he escorted her outside with Reid and Allegra.

"Congrats on surviving the first family dinner," Allegra

joked. "We almost made Drake cry at his."

"That was pretty funny," Bree laughed. "You got off pretty light."

"I'll pick you up at seven, sis." Reid kissed her cheek as Logan opened the door for her. Reid started down the steps and slowly moved his pointer finger back and forth, making it clear Bree was off limits.

Bree watched Logan walk around the car and tapped her foot nervously. Through the whole dinner, she was waiting for him to make a mistake so she could point to a reason to distance herself. But he never gave her one. Instead, every story and every insight gave her more and more reason to be drawn to him.

All the way to her townhouse, she tried to think of reasons to step back. But when he pulled his car into her small driveway, she knew she wouldn't. She had fallen for Logan Ward, and it was time to face it head on. She hoped her heart would survive it.

"Thank you for driving me home. Would you like to come in for a drink or something?" Bree asked with more confidence than she felt.

She was around men all the time and now she understood what they had meant about dating not being easy. They all complained about how hard it was to meet someone and now that she had to ask, she couldn't imagine the courage it took to approach someone and ask for a date. Men were a lot stronger than she gave them credit for.

"That would be great. Let me get the door for you." Logan hopped out of the car with his heart pounding. All the way there he'd tried to think of a way to spend more time with

Bree yet cursed himself for not taking advantage of the time alone to talk more.

He opened the door and held out his hand. She placed hers in his and looked into his eyes. Logan could see the nervousness and the anticipation reflected in them. She was vulnerable and powerful all at once. Knowing he was doing that to her stopped him in his tracks. She deserved someone who could go all in—someone who would not only be there for her the next morning but also be there every morning thereafter. His heart leapt at the idea, but his brain backpedaled. In no more than a week, Logan was going to be back in England. The thought of some other man with Bree was suffocating.

Bree led him to her door and then fumbled with the keys. "Here, let me." Logan took the keys and unlocked the door.

He followed Bree into the cool hallway and placed the keys on the side table. The house was narrow and deep. A couple of feet away was a set of stairs leading to the upstairs bedroom and beyond that, a wide room. A soft cream-colored couch and light blue chairs sat on a red rug in the living room. A large window overlooking the street took up most of the front wall. Behind the living room was an open dining room and the kitchen.

Bree headed for the kitchen and pulled out a bottle of wine. "Would you like a glass?"

"I'd love one. This is a great space."

"Thanks. I love the way it looks so traditional on the outside, but inside it's contemporary without losing the traditional charm."

Bree handed him a glass and they headed for the couch. Logan felt like an idiot. He could admit that. He felt like a fourteen-year-old boy hoping to get his first kiss. Instead of saying something stupid, he sat down next to her as his mind battled between ravishing her and being a gentleman.

Bree kicked off her shoes and sat on the couch. She watched Logan slowly sit down next to her and wondered what he was thinking. He'd been so quiet. Did she do something to make him lose interest? The thought of it hurt her heart. She was stuck. Stuck between wanting to throw caution to the wind and guarding her vulnerabilities.

"Well . . ." they both started at the same time. Logan grinned and set his glass down on the table. Then he reached up and took Bree's glass out of her hand.

"I know I have to go back to London, but . . ." Logan let out a frustrated breath and Bree held hers not wanting to miss a word he said.

Logan paused. What the hell should he say? I like you? I've only known you a couple days and I can't picture my life without you anymore? Yeah, he was pretty sure that would send her running to the hills. Instead, he did what felt right. He leaned forward and placed his lips on hers. When she sighed and leaned forward, he wrapped her in his arms and pulled her onto his lap. Her soft mouth opened to him and he slid his tongue slowly inside. Sometimes words just got in the way.

Bree's fingers ran through his dark hair and tugged him closer. As he deepened the kiss, the world around them exploded. Glass shattered and rained to the ground around them.

At the sound of the glass breaking, Logan had twisted on the couch and buried Bree in the cushions to cover her body with his. Fear and anger washed over him as the last shards of glass fell to the hardwood floor and splintered into a hundred sparkling pieces. Logan lifted his head and saw a brick lying at his feet. He pushed Bree back as he tried to grab it before she saw it.

"Logan, get off of me. What in the . . . oh my God!" Bree gasped as she looked down at the black-and-white picture of Elle, Bree, and Allegra wrapped around the brick. In red marker it read: *Who will be next?*

Chapter Twelve

"What do you mean, calm down?" Bree shouted at Logan as she paced the kitchen. "Bree, you're understandably upset. All I am saying is you've had a shock and now isn't the time to make rash decisions."

"This is the perfect time to make them. Jeff will never suspect a thing if we strike tonight." Bree chewed on her bottom lip as she plotted her revenge.

"Okay. Let's do whatever it is you're thinking *if* you can prove it was Jeff who threw that brick through your window." Logan crossed his arms over his chest and waited. He saw the gamut of emotions run across Bree's face. She had opened her mouth as if to lay out the evidence only to snap it shut.

"I have a feeling he's the one behind all this." Bree let out a long breath and stopped pacing. "But a feeling isn't enough, is it?"

"No, sweetheart, it's not. I got to see you with your family tonight. They're wonderful, supportive, and understanding. I think it's time you called them and let them know they might be in danger."

Bree groaned. "But it's two weeks from Elle and Drake's wedding. I can't do this to them. She has enough to worry about. I mean, for crying out loud, next Friday

Shirley's hosting the bachelorette party—"

"*Shirley*?" Logan's eyes went wide before a smile broke out across his face. Who in their right mind would let Shirley host a bachelorette party? "I think we need to discuss this. I mean, I know we're not dating, but I don't know how I feel about you going out with Shirley."

"Really?" Bree asked with a shake of her head. "That's what you're worried about?"

"Well, our relationship is so new and I'm sure there will be naked men involved somehow. You haven't even seen me naked yet."

Bree's lips twitched. "Relationship, huh?"

Logan looked very uncomfortable as he looked down at his feet. "I wanted to discuss that with you tonight. But, well, I'm a man of few words."

"Less words, more tongue?" Bree laughed when she thought Logan was sufficiently embarrassed. "I was going to talk to you about it as well. But, considering the circumstances we find ourselves in right now, maybe we should reschedule that talk. First I'm going to take your advice to call Elle and Allegra."

Twenty minutes later, her sisters filled the small kitchen as police and one off-duty Secret Service agent looked over the crime scene. Drake and Logan stood on the other side of the island as Bree filled them in on what happened.

"You should have told me you were poaching workers," Elle said in her best CEO voice. "It's no wonder Jeff is trying to get payback."

"I hate to be the voice of doubt, but we don't know it was Jeff. After all, Bree threatened two men," Mallory pointed out.

"*Threaten* is such a strong word. It was more like I politely informed them of the relevant information I had about them," Bree smirked.

"Knock it off, Bree," Elle said with irritation plain in her voice. "That was not some blasé chat among friends. You knew what you were doing. By not keeping us informed, you've put us in danger as well. You need to grow up and realize there are consequences to your actions."

Bree felt the words like a punch to the stomach. "Grow up? Blackmail is pretty damn grown up. Dealing with threats to my life for the past several months is pretty grown up, thank you very much."

Elle shook her head. "No, it's not. Blackmail is the cowardly way out. The grown-up thing to do was to realize you were out of your depth and ask for help."

"And what would you have done differently? Take over Jeff's company like you did when Chord came after you?"

Allegra stepped forward and held up her hands. "Enough. What's done is done. We need to focus on what we're going to do now."

"I'm getting around-the-clock security for all of you until this has been handled," Drake broke in. "You can handle that, right, Mallory?"

"You can't do that! How am I to go to dress fittings and my bachelorette party with a bunch of men in suits following me around?" Elle asked in horror.

"I don't know, but I'm making it happen. I'm not going to let this ruin our day, and I'm not going to have you in any danger." Drake held up his hand when Elle opened her mouth to argue. "Period." Elle's mouth snapped shut and she glared at her husband-to-be.

"Can you teach me that?" Logan whispered before a wet dishrag landed on his face. He looked up at Bree's glaring face and gave her a wink. A small smile appeared, and he was relieved to see the tension from the argument with her sister had already faded.

"I'll be happy to provide protection personally," Mallory said. "I'll be at those events anyway and it won't look unusual. I'll also call Finn and see if he can look out for Allegra. I don't want to draw any attention that shows we know something is up. This could just be a power play and seeing y'all scrambling in fear would only give him confidence."

Allegra shook her head. "Finn's too busy with the agency and he's not even security. We can't ask him to do that."

Bree shot Elle a look and they shared a quick smile at their younger sister's sudden nervousness. Like that, the fight was over. Even growing up, Elle was the bossy one, Bree the wild one, and Allegra the peacemaker. They kept those roles as they grew up, but they never questioned the love that sisters share—even if they wanted to kill each other every now and then.

Mallory shook her head. "Finn helped out when Elle was in trouble, and I know he'll do it again. One of my guys, even dressed as part of the company, would be noticeable. But you've been hanging out with Finn for months. No one would think twice about him."

"That's right. And you have all those fittings with the models this week for your new campaign. Since Finn is trying to expand the agency's clientele, it would be perfectly normal for him to be holding interviews there," Elle told her sister as she and Bree tried not to laugh. It was clear something was going on there, but Allegra and Finn seemed to be the only two oblivious to it.

"Hey, guys," Damien Wallace, the Secret Service agent who had dated Mallory, said to get their attention. "I'm just an observer here, but from what I saw there were no fingerprints. It's clearly a professional job meant to intimidate. They're sending a message that they're not afraid to go after your family if you don't cooperate. And since I know Elle, I'm assuming Bree's also not going to cooperate with the demands laid out in the green letters."

"That's right," Bree said as she crossed her arms preparing for a fight.

"She certainly isn't," Elle and Allegra said at the same time. They stepped up to flank their sister in a show of support.

"Figured that. Mallory, you can help, right?" Damien asked.

Mallory nodded her head. Bree looked back and forth between the ex-couple. Mallory didn't like to talk about her relationships, but whatever caused this one to end didn't seem to create hostility. "We've got that all covered."

"Good. I've heard from my FBI friends about these tactics before, and these kinds of people usually pursue it to the end."

Damien stopped when the detective from the hospital came over to give his report. Mallory had introduced Damien to him as a friend and had left out his occupation. With a shrug, Detective Gruber let Damien hang around. Gruber seemed just as put out now as he had been when he tried to blame the explosion on Bree. "Yeah, we're finished here. Looks like some teenagers just messing around."

"What?!" everyone said incredulously at the same time.

Gruber looked annoyed as he closed his little notebook. "It's a prank. Kids do it all the time. Just like smashing a mailbox. I'd advise putting up some plastic or something until you can get the window replaced. It's going to rain tonight. I'll have the report ready next week for your insurance company."

Bree watched in complete shock as Gruber turned around and walked out of her house. She looked on with a stunned face as the rest of the group joined, all except Damien who was already pulling out his cell phone.

"I'm calling my friend at the FBI. Even a rookie could see this was more than a prank. This, along with the explosion at your building and the ATF's findings being so drastically different from the detective's, should be enough for the FBI to open an investigation on Detective Gruber. Keep me up to date, and I'll let you know what I can find out." Damien walked out the door as he started explaining the case to his friend.

Bree nibbled on her lower lip in thought. There was a plan starting to form in her head, but she knew her sisters wouldn't like it.

"Bree? I know that look. Whatever it is, don't do it," Elle said with her best older-sister voice.

"Do what?"

"Don't act all innocent. You get that look whenever you think about doing something stupid. You got that look before you toilet-papered Ryan's house in high school after he called you some rather unflattering names in shop class. Then you got that same look when you submitted your office building for consideration for building of the year under the name F. Yeux when the organization hosting the award denied you membership because you're a woman."

Logan hid his laugh behind a cough and Elle just shook her head. "She joined and still holds membership. She told them her name was Francois Yeux from Paris and that 'he' had just moved to Atlanta. The idiots bought it."

Bree's proud grin was contagious and soon everyone was laughing. "Sorry, but that one was pretty funny. As I remember it, Ryan totally deserved it, too," Allegra said, sticking up for Bree.

"He did. And I'm not going to do anything yet. I promise." Bree made an X over her heart and her sisters just rolled their eyes. With Bree they knew *yet* was the key word.

"On that ominous note, I'm taking you home." Drake wrapped his arm around Elle's waist and started pulling her to the door as she lectured on the importance of thinking through your actions.

"I'll go with Allegra tonight to make sure her apartment is secure, and I'll give Finn a call as well. Be safe. I don't think anything will happen tonight. It was most likely just a warning," Mallory told Bree as she gave her a hug. "Please don't do anything stupid."

"Have I ever done anything truly stupid?"

"Yes," Mallory answered instantly. "Logan, you have to watch her."

"My pleasure," Logan grinned as he stepped closer to Bree.

At last the door was closed. Bree stood at her broken window and watched Mallory and Allegra head outside. She may not do what she was thinking of tonight, but a very juvenile plan was taking shape in her head. Sometimes humor was the better path to take than revenge. But when you get both at the same time, well, that was perfection.

"Do you have anything we can put over that?" Logan asked.

"I have a tarp in the garage. If you can put that up outside, I'll rig the inside so I'll know if anyone comes in." Bree opened a cabinet and pulled out a variety of chips.

"Chips?"

"They make a great crunch noise when stepped on. I

once covered Reid's bedroom floor with them. He was sneaking out of the house, and I was getting the blame for it. When he came in through his window, the whole house woke up. What kind of childhood did you have if you didn't do this to your brother?" Bree jokingly asked.

Logan just shrugged. "We didn't really get along. My parents were too interested in social events. They liked to be in the society pages, and I found that constraining. My brother, on the other hand, loved it. I went away to college as soon as I could while my brother stayed in Charleston trying to deflower every debutante he could."

"Well, if there is ever the perfect time to pull off what I'm thinking about, then you'll get a taste of it. In the meantime, let's get this fixed."

Bree ripped open the bag of chips as Logan got started covering the space that used to be her window. As they worked, they talked and she learned more of Charleston and the pressure his parents put on him to run the family company. She was so thankful her family had never believed in that. Instead, her parents gave them the opportunities to explore their passions and encouraged them to do things they loved. Her parents believed if you did what you loved, you'd never work a day in your life. And after her father worked so hard to earn enough money to start his own company, he told them that the old saying was true. He loved his job and his company. He loved it so much he believed he never really worked a day after quitting the railroad.

When Bree sensed Logan didn't want to talk about his parents any longer, she told him stories from her time at college and the pranks she talked her sisters into. She turned serious when he asked about what it was like for her in the construction community.

"It's what I love, so I take the bad with the good. It's taken years to form the group of workers I have on my crews. And it took me showing them I could joke and be one of the guys for them to accept me. I had to pick up a hammer and help out. I had to be tough, but fair. Most importantly, I had to be consistent. Slowly, they loosened up and started trusting me. But it's not like that everywhere. At conventions, most sellers think I'm the secretary or just some dumb blonde arm-candy. It still bothers me, but I try to laugh it off when I can. I have a tendency to go overboard just a little when I can't laugh it off."

"As in F. Yeux?" Logan laughed.

"Exactly."

Logan put the hammer and tacks down on the kitchen table and pulled Bree close to him. "I like the fiery side of you. It makes you interesting." The chips fell to the floor as he held her tight against him. "I think it's time we picked up where we were so rudely interrupted."

Logan felt Bree's breath catch as he captured her lips. When she melted into him, he knew that same fiery nature that prompted her naughty side also drove her passion. The sharp intake of breath when he cupped her breast drove him wild. Logan pushed her further as he rolled her nipple slowly between his fingers. Her hand started to travel boldly down his muscled chest. She pushed and he pushed back harder in a silent and sexy play for control. Logan scooped her up placed her on the couch. Gaining control would be a rush, but he knew losing it would be even more special. So special he wondered if he'd be able to walk away from it when the time came to go back to London.

Bree woke up the following morning with her body encased in Logan's warm embrace. Her head lay on one of his arms. The other was draped over her body and cupping her bare breast.

She closed her eyes in embarrassment. They'd made out like teenagers on her couch for most of the night. Even though they had both wanted more, they had sensed that the full action would be too much too soon. Instead, they explored each other with their eyes, hands, and mouths. Now as he stirred next to her, she had no idea what to do. Their chemistry was so powerful it scared her. She was brave, she had courage, but did she have enough to give it all to someone who was leaving? And the better question was, if she did, would she survive when he left?

Chapter Thirteen

B ree stood at the door and watched the doctor write
something on Marcus's chart before heading toward
her. He opened the door and she stepped out of his
way.

"Is it okay for me to see him, doctor?"

"Yes, ma'am. But try to keep it short. He just finished
some physical therapy and is in quite a bit of pain. I gave
him some medicine to help him rest and it should kick in
soon."

Bree gave a nod of understanding and took a deep
breath. She felt like someone was tying her stomach in
knots when she thought about what Marcus was going
through. Reminding herself it wasn't about her, she turned
the knob to his rehab room and tried to paste on a happy
smile.

"Good morning," she said as she came to Marcus's bed.
His color was still pale and he'd lost quite a bit of weight
over the past two weeks. Bree had been coming to see him
three times a week since the accident and sneaking him
snacks. She also knew that her mom came by twice a week
as well to talk with him.

"Hey, Bree. What did you bring me today?" Marcus
asked with a hint of a smile.

"A chocolate hammer and screwdriver," Bree said

proudly as she pulled the miniature chocolates out of her purse.

"Yum. I need a chocolate fix. I just got back from therapy. It's more like torture than a workout." Marcus grunted in pain as he shifted to sit up more in bed.

"A little torture now and a lot of gain later. I heard that the prosthetic they measured you for should be ready soon. Hopefully, that will help a lot."

Marcus looked away from her and took a deep breath. "I'm sure it will. Thank you so much for your kindness."

"Marcus, please. You know you're like family to me. You saved my life. There's nothing I wouldn't do for a friend like you," Bree said sincerely.

Marcus swallowed hard. "You're the best friend anyone could have, Bree. More than I deserve, that's for sure."

"Deserve? Please. You're smart, hardworking, fair to the crew, and loyal. We're the lucky ones here. Now tell me how therapy went." Bree sat back and listened to Marcus's funny story of his hot physical therapist he believed to be the daughter of the devil. By the time she left, Marcus seemed in better spirits as he drifted off to sleep. Bree felt hopeful that he was slowly recovering—physically and mentally.

Logan hung up the phone and stood numbly by his hotel window. It had been almost a week since the night he and Bree had spent together. When they awoke the next morning, everything had seemed perfect on his end. Except for the fact Bree had become skittish. It was as if she were purposefully putting distance between them. Instead of fighting it, Logan had planned romantic dates every night where they talked and laughed. Her skittishness had slowly turned into her breasts pressing against his chest as they said goodnight in a way that didn't involve words. He'd felt her distance evaporating and her passion trying to break free. And over the week she had come to mean more to him than any woman ever had. She was determined, smart, funny . . . and just perfect.

Tonight he had plans to bring her back to his hotel and show her how much she had come to mean to him — all without words. Bree was so used to being in control, she tamped down all emotion and feeling. It made sense to him, even if Bree didn't realize she did it. On the job, she had to be strong. She had to fight the stereotype that women were led by their emotions. So Logan feared if he shared his heart with her, she would have to face hers. He didn't know if Bree was quite ready to be vulnerable enough to expose her emotions.

But it didn't seem that it mattered anymore. He had just been ordered to come back to London with a stopover in New York City to check on a project there. He had to leave that afternoon.

Bree sat looking at the designs for a future project she was interested in bidding on as she found her mind wandering to Logan. Since spending the night together, they'd been dancing around each other. Well, she'd been doing some fancy footwork at least. Logan was just content to stand by and watch her fumble around. He'd taken her to dinner. Then they'd gone for a walk or sat on the porch and talked deep into the night. Logan had pulled back and hadn't pressed when it came to their relationship. The one night together was life changing, but it was also scary. She knew without a doubt that Logan was what her mother had always described as "the one." But knowing he was heading back to London soon was enough to prevent her from having the relationship talk. She didn't think her heart could handle it—even if that meant she was a coward.

The sound of laughter reached her ears a moment before Allegra and Finn walked into her office. "Hey, you two. How were the fittings and interviews with the models?"

Allegra's face lit up even more. "It was amazing. Finn signed five models."

Finn looked proudly at Allegra. "But it was Allegra who casually mentioned that I was there when they started talking about the difficulty they were having standing out from the pack at their big agencies."

Allegra was practically bouncing. "Finn told them how the agency is more like a family. It really hit home for many of these young girls. Nowadays, runway is like the minor leagues and lots of teenagers do them for free or very little money."

"Listen to my little sister sounding all sporty," Bree teased.

"It is! It's just like sports. Finn was telling me all about how much minor league players work and how little they get paid. It's only the few who get called up to the big leagues who start to pull in the money. It's so similar to the modeling world. Even after a model hits the magazine covers, it's all about the endorsements. Just like in sports. And Finn knows all about branding, marketing, and he seems to really understand how modeling and sports go together perfectly. He's already in talks for a commercial with Kane Royale and one of the models for a major fragrance company," Allegra explained excitedly.

Bree was impressed. Finn had really innovated the agency concept and done it in Simpson's style . . . with a family feel. "That's fantastic, Finn."

"Thanks, Bree. Elle was really excited about the direction of the company when we met this morning. I'm just happy I can make her proud after all she's done for me."

Allegra leaned in and lowered her voice. "But the real reason we're here is to find out about you and your hunk." Allegra wriggled her perfectly sculpted eyebrow and Bree blushed. "Oh! So that's how it is."

"About time, too," the call came from down the hall. Everyone shook their heads as they waited for Shirley to stop eavesdropping with her super-charged hearing aids and make her way to the office.

"I only met him once, but he seemed liked he was looking out for you," Finn started to say before all words died. Shirley walked in with a banner hanging across the front of her walker that said *Men are like chocolate; they're never around when you have a craving.*

Shirley stopped and sank into the chair in front of Bree's desk. "I should see if he wants to come out with us tonight for the bachelorette party. I bet he'd look real nice in a hard hat and nothing else."

Allegra just laughed and Bree groaned. "Aw, look at how she blushes, Shirley. It's so cute," Allegra teased.

"I'm feeling out of place here," Finn mumbled.

"Oh, pish-posh," Shirley clucked. "You've got nothing to be ashamed of in that department either. I just can't say anything or Elle will make me go to another one of those sexual harassment seminars. But Mr. Hard-Hat-Cute-Ass doesn't work for Simpson Global anymore."

Bree froze. "What do you mean, he doesn't work for Simpson Global anymore?"

Shirley looked around at their stunned looks. "You don't know? No, I can see you don't. He turned in the final plans to Elle early this morning to give to you. His company is calling him back to London today."

"Why didn't he give them to me?" Bree asked, painfully aware of how pathetic that sounded to the group.

Shirley shrugged. "I think it was some misplaced sense of doing right since he was in a relationship with you. He didn't want anyone saying you approved the design simply because you are doing the nasty."

"But we only did it once!"

"Now that is a shame. If I were younger, he'd still be tied to my bed. But with this arthritis I just can't get the knots as tight as they need to be anymore," Shirley told them as she held up her hands.

Finn cleared his throat. "I'm sorry to hear Logan is leaving. But even with the extra men and the finalized plans, do you think you'll make your milestone?" Finn asked, changing the subject as quickly as he could.

Bree absently nodded. "I think so. I better go see how they are doing. Todd seems to have things under control, though."

"Wait," Allegra said with a touch of concern in her voice. "What about the threats?"

"It's been quiet, but only a couple of the extra men I hired have started. It was all I needed for the demo crew. That's another reason I should go. The extra fifty men I hired away from Jeff started this morning." Bree stood and grabbed her new pink hard hat and numbly headed out of the office.

Logan put the last of his clothes in his suitcase and zipped it closed. He sat staring at the hotel room he'd been staying in for the past two weeks. Instead of relief at the prospect of going home, he felt dread. He needed to tell Bree he'd been called back to London, but right now that was the last thing he wanted to do.

Instead of picking up the phone, he headed to the window to look out at the corporate center. It was like a hive of worker bees swarming. The extra crew members had arrived that morning and immediately went to work welding, framing, and hammering. In just the few hours they'd been there, the building had started to take on life again. Logan felt a sense of pride as he looked at it. Bree could do it. She'd get it done on time and save the project. She might have pissed off some very powerful people, but she hadn't run to hide or played the victim card. No, she had stared adversity down and given it the finger.

The only thing that kept Logan staring out the window and not heading to the airport was that he couldn't shake the feeling Bree was still in danger. It had been quiet recently, but had it been too quiet? He'd only caught glimpses of the person Mallory had put on Bree for protection. Most of the time, Mallory had been around after she'd made sure Elle was ensconced at work.

But Logan had a nagging feeling he shouldn't leave, that it wasn't over. Or was it the fact he didn't want things to be over before they'd given their relationship a real chance? As if fate were answering, he saw a pink hard hat walking through the crowd of workers. Now was the time to find out if he should get on that plane or not. It all depended on the woman wearing that pink hat.

Bree shook her new site manager's hand and smiled. He seemed like a good enough guy, even though he had been one of Jeff's top men. The work that he'd gotten done in the last week was admirable. The cleanup was complete, and the new men who had been brought in on recommendation from some of her own workers seemed to be fitting into her crew without problem.

She was relieved to see work was progressing quickly and most of the men were laughing and talking as they worked. A happy workplace was a productive workplace.

"It appears to be a good transition. Have we had any problems?" Bree asked.

"None. We're all happy to have better-paying jobs with the freedom to come to our boss and have our voices heard. Respect goes a long way on a work site, and your respect for us has us eager to meet your goals," Todd explained as he walked her through the site, showing the improvements.

"Bree!"

Bree turned around and saw Logan picking his way through the crowd. Her heart sped up until she remembered this was the last time she'd see him. Then it crashed to a stop. "Logan? What are you doing here? Shouldn't you be on a plane?"

Logan's step faltered and Bree figured he thought she wouldn't know he was leaving. But he didn't have Shirley and her hearing aids.

"You know," he stated slowly.

Bree could only nod.

Logan looked around and saw Todd take a step back to join a group of her men, including Big Al. They all seemed to pick up on the tension and had stopped working to gather around their boss.

Logan stepped closer so he could lower his voice and not be overheard. "I'm sorry, Bree. My boss is demanding I go to New York this afternoon and then to London in two days. I don't want to leave."

"You have to go. I understand," Bree said as she tried to smile.

"No, you don't understand. I've enjoyed my time with you, and I know there's so much more for us."

Bree was embarrassed by the tears threatening to spill from her eyes. Over the past couple of weeks, her animosity for the unknown Logan Ward had turned to affection — affection she had never felt for anyone before. And now it was set to walk away from her.

"*Que sera sera,* right? My mother always taught me if it's meant to be, then it will be. Obviously we were just not meant to be. But it's been a pleasure to know you, Logan. Not only did you save my life, you showed me a little about life I didn't know before. Thank you."

"Bree. Don't. It's not over. Our time has not run its course."

"Sometimes life just gets in the way of what could have been. Goodbye, Logan. I'm a better person for having known you."

Bree turned and disappeared behind the wall of men. Logan stood staring after her as she picked up a hammer and disappeared inside the building.

Bree swung hard and drove the nail into the wall. Sweat trickled down her back and her ivory silk shirt stuck to her as she grabbed another nail. Her black dress pants were covered in dirt and dust as she worked with her men. The anger, hurt, and disappointment of what might have been was worked out with every swing of the hammer.

The men hadn't said a word when she picked up the hammer and started working. They all seemed to know better. Time passed quickly, and she pretended to not notice that Logan would be in New York by now.

A slow whistle filled the air and everyone glanced behind them. "When I heard you were hammering with the men, this is not what I pictured."

Bree felt a smile tug on her lips. Shirley was in Big Al's arms and clearly enjoying it. "What are you doing, Shirley?"

"It's almost time for the bachelorette party, and I'm your designated driver. Thank goodness your mom sent an extra set of clothes." Shirley held up a micro mini skirt and a shirt that would barely cover her breasts. The men around her turned red and suddenly all had to cough or clear their throats.

"My *mother* sent that?"

"Heavens no. Your mother sent some awful business suit. I left it at the office, but it was a good idea, so I stopped and picked this up for you."

Bree just laughed. She laughed because it was all she could do not to cry. "Okay, Shirley. I put myself in your capable hands."

Chapter Fourteen

What the hell had she been thinking when she trusted Shirley? Bree looked at herself in the mirror with wide unbelieving eyes as Shirley stood behind her smiling. The skirt barely covered her butt. The scarf-like top tied around her neck and had flowing ruffles that covered her breasts . . . barely. Her midriff was left exposed and her legs were on display in bright-red spiked heels.

"I look like a hooker."

"But a very expensive hooker," Shirley said happily. "Now let's go hook some men!"

Shirley held open the door to the restroom in the club and pushed her out. Shirley had reserved the VIP area of the most exclusive dance club in Atlanta. Bree's mother had protested, Allegra and Cousin Mary had loved it, and Elle was resigned to her fate.

"You look amazing!" Allegra squealed.

"She looks like a trollop!" Margaret screeched in dismay.

"Wow, Bree. You were always a tomboy. Who knew you had boobs?" Mallory grinned as she entered the VIP area in tight leather pants and a red lace tank top.

"Yeah, you're going to have to beat the men back with Elle's stilettos," Mary teased as she pointed to the super-sexy shoes Elle had already kicked off.

Everyone stopped talking when one of the hottest men they had ever seen walked up to their group and smiled. Shirley cursed under her breath, her mother fanned herself, Allegra giggled, Mary's mouth fell open, and Elle started to fidget with her engagement ring.

"Hi. I'm Aiden and I noticed you when you walked in. Would you like to dance?" Bree looked around and all the women except Elle were nodding their heads. Was he talking to her?

"Aren't you a looker? I bet I could wash clothes on your stomach," Shirley said as she whistled.

Aiden's eyes twinkled with amusement and he stepped over to Shirley and Bree. "If this lady agrees to dance with me, I'll show you," he whispered to Shirley.

Bree felt a hand to her back and was pushed forward into Aiden's arms. "She's all yours, sonny."

Bree tried to scramble back in mortification, but she felt Aiden's amused laughter as he held her to his chest. With a wink, he lifted up his tight V-neck shirt. She heard a gasp and looked down at the most chiseled abs she'd ever seen. She could bounce a quarter off that! Bree was pretty sure her mother collapsed in a fit of vapors while Shirley snapped a picture.

Bree was still staring when she felt him lead her to the dance floor. He was totally different from Logan. While they were both about the same height, Logan was more natural in his body. Aiden seemed to be made from the minds of a plastic surgeon and physical trainer. When she looked up at his perfect, blinding white teeth, even tan, and complete lack of wrinkles, she felt he wasn't real. Somehow his personality, while nice, seemed to be the same.

On the other hand, Logan was genuine. He flattered her

because he liked to see her roll her eyes. But he also told it like it was. Logan's six pack and legs showed him to be the athlete that he was. And when he smiled, his eyes crinkled in the sexiest way. As Bree looked at Aiden, she didn't think anything could crinkle, wrinkle, or move on his face. She saw her reflection in his completely chemically smoothed forehead.

"It's such a relief to find you here tonight. I didn't know the agency had sent someone else and the thought of handling this crowd by myself is daunting," Aiden told her as his body fell into the rhythm of the dance.

"Sent me here?" Bree asked. Handle what crowd? Bree looked around at the filling nightclub. Sure, there were a lot of young men and women filling the place, but what was there to handle?

"Yeah, for the party. I thought Barry was my backup. But who knows, they could swing both ways." Aiden shrugged as his hand went down to squeeze her bottom. "Nice. We can definitely work with that."

Bree stopped dancing and stepped away. "I'm confused. Work with what and for whom?"

"The old lady up there. She hired two escorts for the bachelorette party. You're with Elite Elegance, aren't you?"

"Oh my God. You think I'm an escort?" Bree gasped and pulled her skirt down as far as she could.

"Aren't you?" Aiden asked, confused.

"I'm the bride's sister," Bree said before mumbling, "Shirley was right."

"Eww, sorry. You're really smokin' hot, though. You could make some serious bills with Elite."

Strangely, this brought a smile to Bree's face. She worked so hard to be sexless that it was nice to be appreciated as a woman. "Thanks, Aiden. I'm doing pretty well at my job now, but I'll keep it in mind if the company ever folds."

"You should. Here's my card."

Bree took it and slid it into her bra. Oh God, she really did look like an escort.

"You want to tell me what's going on?" Aiden asked as he pulled her back into the dance.

"What makes you think anything is going on?" Bree tried to sound nonchalant, but by the way Aiden tried to move his eyebrow, she could tell she wasn't fooling anyone.

"I'm a stranger that you'll never see again. I only know your name is Bree. Take this moment to spill your guts with no judgment."

Bree let out a long breath. Why not? He already thought she was an escort. Could he really think any worse of her? "I met this guy."

"Shouldn't you be happy?"

"He was here only for a couple weeks. I feel like a ninny for liking him so much. Then he had to leave and go back home. I broke it off completely. No texts, no phone calls, no long-distance relationship, and now I feel . . . empty."

Aiden tried to frown, but it came out looking like duck lips. "That's tough. I have just one question. Why didn't you fight for it?"

Bree stopped dancing as Aiden gently stroked her arm in a calming manner. "I was scared," Bree admitted on a whisper.

"You strike me as a woman who doesn't run from something that scares her. Somehow I see you beating it into submission. So why run now?"

Bree looked up at Aiden's smooth face and almost crumbled. "I ruined it. I finally found someone and I ruined it."

"Shhh. If it's love, then it doesn't just disappear. Now you just need to fight for it. And I'd place my money on you." Aiden looked up at the door and then gave her a squeeze.

"And there's Barry now. I'll be happy to escort you home later tonight, "Aiden tried to wink before waving Barry down.

"Thank you for listening, but I think I need a drink." Bree didn't feel any better as she headed to the bar before hiding behind her mother and watching Aiden and Barry make a Mary sandwich.

Elle and Mallory pulled to a stop in front of Bree's house and looked at the new window. They were all in a state of shock. The image of Shirley, Aiden, and Barry . . . it was all too much.

"Well," Elle started. "That was certainly . . . memorable."

Bree snorted and Mallory tried to fight the laughter causing her shoulders to shake uncontrollably. "Memorable is one way to put it," Bree said as she almost fell out of the door.

"Hey, why don't you come home with me tonight? I don't like the idea of you staying here by yourself," Elle said, quickly changing to big sister mode.

"I'm fine." Bree waved her off before tripping on the curb and taking a facer into the azalea bushes. She felt hands grabbing at her before she was pulled from the attacking bush. "Maybe staying at your house wouldn't be such a bad idea," Bree conceded before being tucked back into the car.

"Does this sudden desire to drink enough vodka to

drown a horse have anything to do with a certain man leaving for London?" Mallory asked as she pulled away from the curb and headed to Elle's house.

"Nah. It has to do with being mistaken for an escort . . . and a certain guy heading to London in a couple hours," Bree ended quietly. It was supposed to be a fun night. She didn't want to think about her heart breaking.

Elle wrapped her arm around Bree's shoulder. "Does it hurt?"

Bree just nodded. Cosmo-flavored tears slowly fell from her eyes. "It shouldn't hurt this badly. I've only known him a couple weeks."

"Love doesn't follow a time frame, Bree."

"I don't." Hiccup. "Love him." Hiccup.

"You used to be such an accomplished liar," Elle tried to tease.

Bree felt the tears coming faster as she laid her head on her sister's shoulder. "I tried not to fall in love. I really did. I even knew he was going to leave. But, some part of me hoped he wouldn't and that's the part of me who's broken-hearted."

"You didn't have to sever all ties, you know. Take the plane and visit him," Mallory encouraged.

"No." Bree shook her head. "If I see him, he'll be perfect. Nice, funny, pushy, supportive, sexy, and I'll want him even more. It's better to cut it off cold turkey. The pain of a broken heart will heal eventually."

"Then we won't talk about him anymore. Unless you bring it up," Elle added quickly.

Bree shook her head. As Elle led her to the guest room, she tried to think of anything other than the man who had flown to London with her heart.

Logan set his bags down in his flat and looked around for the first time in a month. It was strange being back. And suddenly this place that had been his sanctuary for the past ten years didn't seem like home anymore.

He'd managed to get the work in New York done even with his mind stuck on Bree. The feeling of having made a colossal mistake weighed him down as he collapsed onto his couch. Was this worth it? He looked around at his luxury flat and his bags sitting at his feet. His job at Clarke Group was what he'd worked hard to achieve. But the pride he had in his position was gone. Maybe it was just because it was so late at night and he'd been traveling all day. Or maybe it was because his priorities had changed since the last time he was home.

Logan picked up his cell phone and scrolled to Bree's number. It was Sunday night in London, so only Sunday afternoon in Atlanta. He could call to see how the bachelorette party went. No, Bree made it clear she didn't want to talk to him. Instead, he scrolled down and hit the Call button.

"Hello, sweetheart. How's my favorite lady doing this morning?"

"I would be doing better if you'd called sooner."

"Sorry. I just got home. How's everything going? I've missed you."

"I just bet you have. I must admit I've missed those sweet buns of yours, too."

Logan laughed. "It's really good to hear your voice."

"It would be better if you were here in person."

Logan picked up on the hint and sighed. "I wish I were, Shirley. How is Bree?"

Chapter Fifteen

"You can't come in here, Mr. Henderson!"

Bree looked up from the paperwork on her desk as Noah tried to block Jeff from pushing his way into her office. What a fabulous way to start this Monday morning.

Bree set her pen down and kept her eyes on Jeff. He was breathing hard and his normally calm face was red. "What the hell do you think you're doing stealing my workers?"

"I didn't steal them. I just made them a better offer. That's business, isn't it?" Bree crossed her legs and sat back in her black leather chair.

"Dirty business!" Jeff slammed his hands on her desk and glared.

Bree shrugged. "I learned it from you. And, Jeff," Bree leaned forward keeping her eyes on his, "it's not nearly as bad as you trying to kill me."

"You're going to regret this," Jeff hissed.

Bree just smiled. "Somehow I don't think so. You may be able to pay off the local police, but you forget I have friends, too."

This time Jeff didn't try to deny it. He didn't try to bullshit her. He didn't try to smile his way out of it. But he also didn't admit anything. Instead he took a deep breath and pushed back away from her desk.

"You're out of your league, darlin'." With a slow smile that sent chills down Bree's back, Jeff turned around and walked out of her office.

She heard Jeff curse and then a *thump* as the floor shook. Bree leaned so she could see out the door and saw Shirley slowly make her way by on her walker. She looked at Bree and winked. Bree fell back against her chair and found her hands shaking but a smile on her face. Shirley had tripped the bastard with her walker.

Jeff still hadn't given her any evidence to use against him. However, it also didn't appear he was trying to deny any involvement either. If only Damien's FBI contact could take over the investigation, then she'd feel safer. Bree picked up her phone and dialed an extension. "Hi, Mary. Will you look into all the charity events Mr. Westin is attending and bring them to me, please?"

"Mallory, it will be perfect," Bree said for the hundredth time. "I won't say a thing to him about you."

Mallory held the fancy gold-encrusted envelope in her hand and refused to let it go. "No."

It had occurred to Bree that Jeff was the big fish in the pond of Atlanta. What she needed to get him rattled was a bigger fish in a bigger pond. When Mary dropped the society page of that morning's paper on her desk and smiled, Bree had her answer. Pictures were worth a thousand words. And on the front of the society page was none other than Georgia's U.S. senator, Claudel Westin. Bree knew him as Mallory's father.

"Please. He'll be at the Charity for the Arts ball tonight.

All I need is a couple pictures with him. I don't even have to tell him who I am," Bree begged.

"Can't you get your own invitation? Lord knows you have enough money," Mallory complained.

"I do, but this is an old society event. The Simpsons, no matter how much money we have now, are not old society. I was not a debutante. I was not launched into society. I do not move in those circles. Which is why I need your invitation."

Mallory may not act like it when she carries her gun at her back and her knife in her sexy boot, but those were her grandmother's pearls around her neck. She also had the Westin name and, in Georgia, that meant something. It meant her great-great-great-granddaddy had been one of the first governors of Georgia. It meant her great-great-great-grandmother was a founding member of the Daughters of the South. It meant her great-great-grandmother had welcomed the King of England to their plantation because he'd enjoyed their peaches so much. It meant that her great-grandfather was a war hero who brought pride to the state for his heroics, and it meant her grandfather and father had both served in politics. Her grandfather had been an ambassador and her father was a career politician, having been in the U.S. Senate for the past twenty-five years and counting. And it meant Mallory received an invitation to every single society event in the entire state of Georgia. To have a Westin at your event improved things instantly. But it was also Mallory, which meant she was never the Westin at any of the society events.

"To even use this invitation will only encourage them to send me more," Mallory complained as she reluctantly passed it over to Bree.

"You'll be buried in them tomorrow, but it will be worth it when my picture is on the front page of the paper with our state's beloved senator. Jeff will have to think twice about all the contacts he has." Bree took the invitation and looked at the perfect script.

"Hmm. We'll see how this goes. But don't you dare tell my daddy what I've been doing, or who I've been dating, or anything!"

"I won't, but why not?"

Mallory just waved the question away. "The better question is: do you have a gown? This is a full society shindig and the bigger the better — hair, jewels, and dresses — there is no such thing as too big."

Mallory grabbed Bree's hand and they disappeared into the depths of Mallory's spare room closet.

Bree flipped the train to the dark blue, strapless satin gown behind her. She'd applied dark eye shadow mixed with deep blues to match the dress and her eyes. Her strawberry blonde hair hung straight down her back after being slicked back against her temples and teased up on top. Overall, it was a very dramatic effect.

She walked up the stairs and handed the invitation to one of the tuxedoed men at the door before going inside. Photos were snapped as people danced and talked around her. Bree kept an eye out for Senator Westin's silver hair as she circled the room.

With a smile, she grabbed a glass of champagne and headed for her target. She found him talking to this evening's host and hostess with an army of reporters documenting every second. She was going to slip over there, give him a quick hug that would be documented by the papers, and then casually suggest to one of her friends who happens to run one of the Atlanta papers that she should put this picture on the front page. Easy-peasy.

Bree grabbed an extra glass of champagne and walked to the senator's side. "Here's the champagne you wanted, sir. I have to say, it's wonderful seeing you again." Bree leaned forward and kissed each of his slightly wrinkled cheeks as the cameras flashed.

Senator Westin automatically complied with the greeting and kissed her cheek as well. He took the glass of champagne and thanked her. Bree had to admit she was curious. She hadn't seen Mallory's father in, well, ever. Mallory never invited anyone to her childhood home. Elle had gone once and said the plantation was beautiful, but nothing more. Then it just seemed Mallory had become a mainstay at the Simpson house. Being a young teenager, Bree never thought anything of it. Which is why she was surprised when Senator Westin took the glass of champagne out of her hand and handed it to an aide.

"Miss Bree Simpson. I've been waiting for the dance you promised me," he said loud enough for the reporters and gossips hanging around to hear.

Bree almost dug in her silver Prada heels, but instead she plastered on her best happy face and let the senator escort her onto the dance floor.

"It's always nice to meet one of my daughter's friends. Is Mallory here with you tonight?" Bree looked at Mallory's father. He was in his late fifties but carried the years very well. The senator wasn't like most of the men in Washington. He rode horses, shot guns, and ran every morning. The easy way he glided Bree around the floor also told her he hadn't forgotten his mandatory childhood dance lessons.

"No, she's not, and how do you know who I am?"

Senator Westin chuckled. "I'm on the intelligence committee. I'm not blind. Do you not think a father would keep tabs on the girl his daughter practically lived with when she was younger?"

"I got the impression you didn't care what Mallory did."

"Of course I care. She's a Westin. She's *the* Westin heiress. Not that you would ever understand societal pressures."

Bree laughed as if she hadn't just received a polite jab to her social standing. "You're right. Thank goodness. I spend my spare time picking lint out of my bellybutton. I'm surprised I can even dance my way across the floor, which you do quite wonderfully."

"Very nicely played, Miss Simpson. Is my daughter still dating that boring Secret Service agent? At least he's a step up from the state trooper," Senator Westin said as he tried to hide his distaste.

"I'm sorry. My sister is closer to Mallory than I am. I don't have all the details of her life. It may seem like a crazy idea, but if you want to know, why not just ask Mallory?" Bree executed a small curtsey as the song ended and with one last smile walked away from the senator.

"I would if she'd talk to me," was the last thing she heard from the senator before the music started again.

Logan stared at his bags sitting at the foot of his bed. He'd been home for two days and couldn't bring himself to unpack. He couldn't do a lot of things, actually. He wasn't sleeping much, which was why he was still awake in the early morning hours. He couldn't put down his phone, which was why it was still in his hands. And he couldn't focus on work, which was why he had taken the rest of the week off.

Work had been a disaster. He'd made a bunch of calls and caught up on his emails but didn't remember a second of it. Instead, he'd been thinking about Bree and thinking of the house he'd design for them.

Logan had thought about the bedroom they'd share, the nursery their children would occupy just down the hall, and his home office connected by French doors to Bree's matching office. It all seemed right. So he had started sketching. And when he finished the sketch, the workday was over. He'd called his boss and told him he must have caught something in the States and needed the week to recover.

When he made it home he'd started picturing the houses of happy couples, houses, and relationships he wished he had with Bree. He picked up his sketchbook and started drawing. The ideas flowed. The excitement of building a house for someone to love and experience life in filled him with a nervous happiness. This is what he should be doing. This is what had been missing from his life — Bree and the ability to design what he wanted to. Houses that spoke of love, commitment, and growth — houses that were the true heart of a family. Just as Bree was for him.

He worked all night sketching. It was why he was still up at five in the morning when his phone rang.

Chapter Sixteen

Bree held up the edge of her dress and slid behind the wheel of Reid's sports car. The music from the gallery could still be heard floating on the air. She looked in her rearview mirror and saw the familiar lights of the SUV Mallory's man drove. After a week of quiet days and nights, Bree had thought she didn't need the security anymore. However, after Jeff stormed into her office that morning, she was glad he was there.

The traffic was light this late at night. Bree was able to get out of downtown and onto the interstate with little trouble. She'd even talked to her friend at the paper while driving and was assured the picture of Bree and the senator would be on the front page of the paper tomorrow morning.

Bree hung up the phone as she approached her exit. Slowing down on the ramp, she stopped at the light and waited to turn left. While waiting, Bree couldn't help but think of Logan. She wanted to call him. She wanted to tell him what happened today. She wanted to share her thoughts and feelings at having met Mallory's father. She wanted to hear how his day went. Maybe Mallory had been right. She should have tried to make it work.

"I'm so stupid!" Bree chided herself as she pressed on the gas and shot from the stop line when the light turned green. She was going to call Logan as soon as she got back to the house. Or maybe she'd just get on the plane and go see him. Bree had to explain to him how much he'd come to mean to her. She hadn't even realized it at first, but the way he listened, the way they joked, the way her heart was full of him, all showed how much she'd fallen in love with him.

Bree was so caught up in her thoughts she didn't notice the headlights until it was too late. The impact of the SUV crushed her door. She couldn't even scream as her body was hurled to the right, only to be snapped back and slammed into the airbag covering her door. The seatbelt burned into her neck as it caught and refused to go slack. The front airbag deployed almost simultaneously, sending her beaten body crashing back into the seat.

The airbag held her in place as the world continued to spin. She heard her passenger window shatter and the airbag covering it ripped away.

"Help me," she managed in a small voice to the dark figure leaning into the car.

"This is your last warning. You know what you have to do or next time you'll be dead. But first I'll start with your sisters. You'll attend every funeral knowing you're one step closer to joining them if you don't hand off the corporate building job to the other owners by the end of the week."

Bree was hyperventilating. She couldn't draw breath into her lungs, and she couldn't stop the man as he jumped into a waiting car. She heard her security yelling. But it wasn't enough to keep the world from tilting and trying to fade black as she battled for oxygen. Only the pain radiating through her body kept the darkness at bay.

A knife appeared in front of her, but she couldn't scream. Bree was sure the man had come back to finish her off, but instead the airbag was torn away from the steering wheel and her bodyguard's worried face came into view.

"An ambulance is on its way, Miss Simpson. Can you feel your legs?"

Bree tried to nod but ended up hissing in pain instead. "I can feel them," she ended up gasping.

"You're hyperventilating because you're upset. Just keep breathing. Know that the air is flowing into your lungs. Close your eyes and envision the air flowing through your nose and filling your lungs."

Bree closed her eyes and listened to his calm voice. Soon she felt the air and her body relaxed. Unfortunately, it also made her painfully aware of her injuries.

"How are you feeling now?" he asked as the sound of sirens reached her ears.

"Better. I hurt, though. My neck is burning and my shoulder . . ."

"It looks dislocated. It'll hurt like a bitch, but it's not serious. What did the man say to you?"

Bree closed her eyes as she tried to remember. "This was my last warning. He'll come after my family next."

"While they work on you, I'm going to call Mallory and your family. I'll be five feet away."

Bree was worried she was hallucinating as the image of the man dressed as a doctor appeared next to her bed in the Emergency Room.

"Hello, Bree. It's nice to see you again."

"Aiden! If I'm not imagining this, then you better hurry with my exam. Shirley will probably be here soon."

The sight of Aiden going white under his spray-on tan was enough to make her feel better. "I better warn Barry. We're both residents here — me in the ER and him in Plastics. I'd appreciate if, um, you wouldn't mention how we're paying off our student loans."

"Ow!" Bree hissed as Dr. Aiden pressed on her shoulder. "I won't tell if you stop hurting me."

"Then I'm in trouble. Your shoulder is dislocated. Luckily, your knee is just bruised, but we'll X-ray it just to make sure. The pain on your neck you're complaining about is seatbelt burn and you have a mild case of whiplash. Now, I'm going to call in all my favors with every nurse and tech I know to get you into X-ray before Shirley gets here. But first, let's get this incredibly sexy shoulder back into place."

"Any chance you can take off your shirt while you do that?" Bree asked as the pain medicine took effect, allowing Aiden to put her shoulder back in place.

"There," Aiden smiled as Bree took deep breaths, hoping the pain would fade. "Good as new. X-ray time!" he said cheerfully as he hurried her into a wheelchair and started to race her down the hall.

"Bree!" Her mother along with the rest of the family rushed from the ER room and stopped the nurse wheeling her back from where Aiden had looked over her X-rays. "Oh, honey. Are you okay? What did the doctor say? I want to talk to him, where is he?"

"Mom, I'm fine. My shoulder was dislocated, but everything else is fine. No broken bones. Just starting to get really sore and tired. My head seems to be okay, but they're going to keep me overnight just to make sure."

The nurse helped her get into bed and made sure she didn't moon her family. The pain medicine that had made her loopy was now making her tired. All she wanted to do was sleep.

"Well, I want to talk to your doctor anyway. I need to be reassured," Margaret said as she wrung her hands.

"Mom, I think Bree is about to pass out from exhaustion. She's fine. Drake will go find the doctor and get a full report while we say goodnight," Elle said gently as Drake got the message and hurried to get a full report.

Bree managed a soft smile. "Really, Mom. I'm fine. This medicine is just making me sleepy. I'll be at work first thing tomorrow."

"You will do no such thing. You will move back in with me and I will take care of you."

"Mo-o-m," Bree whined, accompanied by an eye roll. "I'm not a kid anymore. I can take care of myself."

Margaret just shook her head. "When will you all learn? You'll always be my babies. And I will always want to take care of you."

Allegra wrapped her arm around her mom's shoulder. "How about you stay for a while tonight so you can see that Bree's all right. Then we'll tackle the care instructions tomorrow after her doctor has checked her out."

Margaret nodded her head and took a seat next to Bree's bed. Bree felt her eyes start to fall.

"Man, Bree. I'm secure enough to admit this. Your doctor is a handsome man," Drake told the women as he sauntered into the room. Bree's eyes shot open. "So you have noticed," Drake teased.

"It would be nice to have a doctor in the family," Elle joked. Bree looked at her sister. When their eyes connected, Bree gave her a look only a sister could interpret. "But then again, they are always so busy. Now an architect . . ."

Bree gave up. She just closed her eyes and figured if she faked going to sleep maybe her family would leave, bless their hearts. But she never found out. The second she closed her eyes, she fell fast asleep.

Bree had a feeling her mom was staring at her before she even opened her eyes. She stretched and almost immediately regretted it. She was so sore that she involuntarily groaned as she moved.

"Is there anything I can get you, sweetheart?"

Bree's brow creased. That wasn't her mom's voice. She opened her eyes and blinked at the light coming in through the window.

"Logan? Is that you or did I hit my head harder than I thought?"

The deep chuckle caused her heart to race. He was here!

"It's me. Your mother called me last night and told me what happened. Your brother was in Paris and ordered the plane to detour to London to pick me up. How are you feeling?"

"Oh," Bree moaned. "I'm pretty sore, but we have to stop seeing each other in the hospital."

Logan's lips quirked and Bree's stomach turned to mush. "I agree. As much as I like taking care of you, I'd rather do it under different circumstances."

The mush turned into flutters as Logan reached out and stroked the side of her face. "How long can you stay?" Bree hated to ask. She should live in the present, but she had to know.

Bree felt so good pressed against his hand. Logan didn't want to think about leaving already, but he knew she had to ask. He had given himself a week to win her heart. If those sparks that he thought were already there weren't, then he'd leave and never come back. But, if they were there . . . "A week. I'll stay through your sister's wedding. I took some long overdue vacation time. I was thinking we could . . ."

Logan looked up as the door to her room opened and her doctor walked in. Holy shit, that wasn't a doctor; that was a freaking male model.

"How ya doing this morning, sexy?" The doctor grinned, kind of, before turning and acting surprised to see Logan sitting there. Logan's hands were clenched and he was thinking some very harmful thoughts toward the doctor. "Oh, you have company."

Bree giggled. *She giggled!* "This is Logan Ward. Logan, this is my doctor, Aiden Starr."

"You've got to be kidding me," Logan said drily. He hadn't even been gone a week and he'd already been replaced.

"Is this *him?*" the doctor whispered to Bree. She nodded and Logan lost it.

"This *him* is leaving to give you two some privacy. Thank you for answering all the questions I had." Logan shot up from his chair and stormed out of the room. He ignored Bree cursing after him and was stabbing the elevator button when he was grabbed from behind.

Logan spun around and knocked Dr. Starr's hands from his shoulders. "What the hell do you think you're doing?"

"Stopping you from making the biggest mistake of your life. Bree's not my girlfriend. We met the other night at her sister's bachelorette party and we talked. About you, mostly."

"Mostly?" Logan asked hesitantly as hope started to build.

Dr. Starr looked a little embarrassed and then leaned forward and lowered his voice. "You can't tell anyone, but this old lady named Shirley hired me to, um, entertain the ladies." When Logan looked confused, Dr. Starr continued. "I'm an escort. I do it on weekends to help pay off my student loan debt. And Shirley had dressed Bree for the night. And I . . . well, um, I thought she was another escort."

Logan didn't know whether to laugh or be mad that this guy thought Bree was an escort. If Shirley dressed her, then he could certainly understand it. Bree had a killer body hidden under her work clothes — a body that he'd thought about constantly. "You thought Bree was an escort?" Logan decided laughter was the way to go.

Dr. Starr looked relieved and smiled. "I even told her she could get a job as one. I mean, she was in a skirt that barely covered her bottom and her butt is *fiiiine*."

Logan must have growled because Dr. Starr stopped and cleared his throat.

"Do you know who Bree is?" Logan asked a little sharper than he meant to.

"No."

Logan laughed this time. "She's Bree Simpson of Simpson Global. Bree is the VP of their steel and construction side."

"Holy crap. I asked a major donor of the children's hospital if she wanted to moonlight as an escort," Dr. Starr groaned as he buried his head in his hands.

"I'm sure she finds it as funny as I do." Logan slapped Dr. Starr on the back. "Now tell me how she's doing."

"After I die of embarrassment." Dr. Starr took a deep breath and shook his head clear. "She's good. She'll be sore the next couple of days and shouldn't stress her shoulder too much. I was about to tell her she could go home. I've had to stay away because her mom was here, and I really didn't want anyone to recognize me from that night."

"I won't say a word. Now, I'll take *my* girl home." Logan shook Dr. Starr's hand and headed back to Bree's room.

"Logan," Dr. Starr called out. "She really likes you. Some women are worth moving mountains for . . . or crossing an ocean."

With a nod of understanding, Logan headed back into Bree's room. He hated what he saw. Bree was yelling through tears at the nurse to hurry and remove the IV.

"Bree. Be quiet and let her do her job," Logan chided kindly.

"Logan! I thought you left."

"I think I better take you home. We have a lot of talking to do. And if we wait too long, your mom will show up and want to take you back to her house. Besides, some of what I want to tell you doesn't involve words."

"Oh my," Bree and the nurse gasped at the same time.

Chapter Seventeen

Logan picked up the paper from Bree's front stoop and carried it inside. It was the only thing Bree had asked for since he brought her home. And now he could see why. There was a picture of her and a Senator Westin dancing on the front page. They were smiling at each other as if they were old friends.

"Is this what you couldn't wait to see?" Logan asked as he handed it to her.

"Oh, that's perfect." Bree smiled up at him.

"I know that twinkle in your eye. What did you do?"

"I went after the bigger fish. I don't think it's Trevor who is behind this. I think it's Jeff. It's just a gut instinct. After I took some of his crew, he visited me and sort of threatened me. And then last night, I was involved in the car accident and given one week to step down from the corporate build. It has to be Jeff. I just can't prove it."

"And so you . . . I don't know. Why are you pictured with some old senator?"

"Because Jeff is the big fish in the Atlanta pond. I needed a bigger fish. Senator Westin is the biggest fish in Georgia. He also happens to be Mallory's father. I wanted to show Jeff that I had contacts, too — big ones. He doesn't have to know that's the first time I really talked to Senator Westin or that we only talked about Mallory. It should still send a message."

Logan shook his head. "So you're putting yourself in even more danger? When he sees this, he's going to go ballistic."

"I know. Isn't it great?"

"How?"

"People mess up more when they're emotional. Ever try to finish plans when you're angry, upset, or sad? It takes twice as long because you usually mess up a couple of times."

Sadly, Logan knew what she meant. But how it translated into catching Jeff, he had no idea. "Just tell me what you need me to do."

Bree blushed and Logan had to remind himself that she was injured. Right now his erection had a mind of its own.

"I need a date for the wedding."

Logan smiled and took her hand in his. "I'd love to. Speaking of weddings . . ."

Bree's phone beeped and she glanced at it quickly. "Oh! Marcus's prosthetic arrived. I know I'm supposed to be resting, but I need to go see how he is. He was really depressed when I saw him last time. He had no color and was very sad until I got him to tell me stories about this physical therapist I think he likes."

"If you eat your meal and feel well enough, I'll take you. But then we need to talk."

"Marcus!" Bree grimaced as she tried to hurry into his room. "How is it?"

Marcus smiled up to her. "It fits perfectly. Of course it's a little uncomfortable since the surgical site is still healing, but I just finished the first round of physical therapy with it and it went pretty well."

"That's fantastic." Bree gave her old site manager a hug but hissed as he squeezed her shoulder. "You remember Logan Ward, right?"

"Barely. I know he brought you after the accident. It's nice to see you when I'm not out of it on painkillers. Al tells me it was you who found me and helped save me."

Logan shook his hand. "That's right. I'm glad you're doing better."

"Thanks. I wasn't for a while. But because of Bree and her mother, I have hope again. I want to know what's going on. What happened to you, Bree?"

"Jeff got a little mad I hired some . . . okay, a lot, of his crew. He sent a thug to crash into me as a warning. I'm okay, though," Bree smiled. How she was feeling should be the last thing Marcus needed to worry about.

"He did what?" Marcus asked with his voice raised. "How do you know it was him?"

"I don't have any evidence, but it's a strong coincidence that after he stormed into my office and told me he'd get even that this happened. Plus the guy who hit me told me I had to step down by the end of the week. It has to be Jeff. He told me he was already talking with the owners. I just wish I had the evidence to put him away for what he did to you and me." Bree took a deep breath. "But, let's not talk about Jeff. I want to hear more about how you are doing."

Marcus fidgeted with the sheet on his bed. "I don't like this, Bree. This shouldn't be happening."

"Marcus. It's okay. I'll handle it. Really, I don't want you to worry. I want you to focus on you."

Marcus shook his head. "No. It's not right. You're a good person. A kind person."

Bree sat down next to him and took his hand in hers. "Marcus, please don't get upset. I promise I'll get justice for you and me both. Now, please, tell me what your doctor said. I bet he's proud of your hard work."

Marcus took a deep breath and looked at Bree's hand holding his. "Okay. I'll let it go for now. The doctor thinks I can go home this week. A physical therapist will come to my house for another month to help me adjust and work on strengthening my leg."

"That's fantastic." Bree smiled at Marcus and then at Logan. She didn't know how, but she was going to fulfill that promise to Marcus and she wouldn't stop until Jeff was in prison.

Logan was growing more frustrated by the minute. He'd wanted to have Bree to himself for a while. He wanted to tell her why he was here this week. He wanted to tell her he loved her. And he really wanted to find out if they could make a relationship work. Instead, as soon as they arrived home, her whole family was waiting for her.

"You're right. We can't let Jeff get away with this," Elle told the group.

"But how can you talk about justice when we don't even know Jeff did it?" Allegra asked. "I know he's an ass, but that doesn't make him guilty. Trevor beats his wife and other women. It wouldn't be out of the realm of possibility for him to order you to be hurt. He clearly has no problem hurting women."

"What a great business you're in, sis," Reid said dryly.

"Like your business is any less shady. Nothing bad ever happens when dealing with celebrities or casinos," Bree shot back.

"Children," Margaret held up her hands. "We're getting off point."

"I took five of Trevor's top workers and he did nothing. Jeff, on the other hand, stormed my office," Bree told them.

Drake shrugged. "You took a lot more than five. Plus, that doesn't mean anything. If you stole my workers I wouldn't storm into your office either. But I would go after you. It's a pretty dirty tactic, Bree."

Bree snapped her mouth shut at the subtle rebuke. She knew it was underhanded. She knew it was wrong, but she'd done it anyway. Righteous indignation had let her ignore that fact. But hearing it from Drake, her future brother-in-law and someone she trusted and respected, made her feel just plain bad.

Logan gently touched her arm. When she looked up, Logan's face was full of concern. "What's the matter, Bree?" he whispered as the others continued debating.

"I can't believe it. I wasn't standing up to them. I became them. I stooped to their level thinking I was doing the right thing for Marcus and me."

"Yes, you did. The real question is what are you going to about it?"

"I don't know if I can fix it."

"I think you can. Trevor Marion is a bad man. He doesn't deserve to breathe for what he does to women. Stop playing his game and play yours. Turn him in and ask the police to take him into custody quietly. Then, if a move is made, that's more evidence that Jeff is behind this."

"I think that's an excellent idea and point, Logan," Margaret said coming up to them. "We love you no matter what you decide to do, Bree. We're your family and we'll support you. The choice of how you want to handle this is

155

yours."

Bree looked at her family all nodding their heads in approval and knew they'd stand by her. Her sister was getting ready for her marriage and she'd put it all on hold if Bree needed her. This was love. This was family. Mallory was right. This path was a hard one to go down and she was through with it. She was ready to handle things her way.

Bree pulled out her cell phone and dialed. "Damien, it's Bree Simpson. Who is the state trooper you play basketball with? I have some evidence he might want to see."

Chapter Eighteen

ogan took off his sports coat and slid it over Bree's
shoulders. She stood quietly shaking with nerves in
the shadows near the lone trooper vehicle in the
upscale neighborhood outside of Atlanta. Damien had
given Bree the best news he could have given her when she
called. The FBI was now investigating members of the local
police force for corruption. Bree had agreed to meet with
Agent Delmont tomorrow morning. But tonight Logan kept
one arm around her as they watched Trooper Floyd knock
on Trevor Marion's door.

Bree had insisted on going. She promised to stay out of
sight, but she had wanted to see for herself that the man
was arrested.

A young girl with lopsided pigtails opened the door as
she cried for all she was worth. The shouts that came from
behind the little girl reached Logan's ears. Trooper Floyd
tossed them a quick look and pointed to the girl before
rushing into the house with his gun drawn and calling for
backup.

"Stay here," Logan ordered Bree as he darted up the
mansion's well manicured lawn. The child, no more than
six, stood at the threshold of the door with a pink teddy
bear clutched to her chest.

"Hi there, sweetie," Logan stopped in front of her and

knelt down. The little girl with big blue eyes looked up him, and he felt his heart break at the sight of a fresh red mark across her face.

"He's hurting my mommy," she cried.

Logan fought back tears as he held out his hand. "The nice policeman is here to stop him from hurting anyone ever again. Can you take my hand, and I'll introduce you to my friend Bree. She just loves teddy bears and would like nothing more than to hear all about yours."

The girl sniffed and looked at Bree. "Smoochy likes nice ladies." She put her small thin hand in his and he smiled at Bree.

"My name is Logan, what's yours?"

"Anna Beth Marion," she answered as tears streamed down her round cheeks.

Logan led her down the steps and across the lawn to where Bree stood, trying very hard to pretend a woman's screams weren't filling the night air.

"Why, hello there. What a cute teddy bear you have." Bree smiled as she knelt down next to Logan behind the safety of the cruiser.

"Thank you," Anna Beth said with a sniff as the sound of a gunshot echoed through the night.

Anna Beth jumped and threw her arms around Logan's neck. Tears soaked his shirt as she clung to him in the sudden silence that followed. His eyes locked with Bree's as he wrapped Anna Beth in his arms. "You're safe, sweetheart," he murmured into her pigtails.

Looking over her little shoulder, Logan kept her head pressed against his chest as a figure emerged from the doorway. Bree stepped in front of them and he was sure she'd fight Trevor to the death to protect this little girl.

Logan leaned around her and saw a second figure emerge.

Trooper Floyd wrapped his arm around the woman and helped her down the stairs and into the cruiser. He hurried to the trunk and pulled out a blanket. Logan saw Bree's body start to shake as she blocked the view of the bloody and battered woman from Anna Beth.

Trooper Floyd talked quietly to the woman and wrapped a blanket around her torn nightgown. The woman stared straight ahead, hardly blinking. Slowly, she turned her head and stared at her house.

"You're safe now, Nikki."

"You're never safe from the devil," Nikki muttered as she kept her eye on the door.

"You are now. You have my word," Trooper Floyd promised.

"I don't believe you. I want to see the body. I want to put another bullet right between his eyes."

Nikki was growing frantic and Trooper Floyd was doing everything he could to keep her calm without touching her. Bree stepped closer. She felt her teeth chattering. All of this was her fault. She'd done this to this family. If she'd turned Trevor in when she got the evidence, then he couldn't have hurt his wife and daughter tonight.

"You cops are all the same! You've been here before. You've seen the abuse and done nothing! You just tell me I'm overreacting. That nothing can be done. My reports get *misplaced* and I'm called *crazy*. And then you threaten to charge me with kidnapping if I take my daughter away from this house." Nikki was breathing deeply and screaming now. Her face was white under the bruises as she looked around frantically. "You've taken her! Where is she? Anna Beth!"

Bree hurried to the car door. "Nikki, Anna Beth is safe. We've been watching her."

"No! Don't take her!" Nikki grabbed the front of the jacket Bree was wearing and wept.

"I'm not going to take her. My friend Logan has her and is trying to keep her safe from seeing all of this. I'm not with the police. I'm the one who brought the police. I'm Bree Simpson."

Nikki's eyes widened and she grew agitated once again. "You have to get out of here. He'll kill you!"

Bree reached around and took her hands in hers. "He'll never hurt anyone again."

Headlights filled the sleepy street as the coroner and more troopers arrived. Anna Beth had been photographed and then Logan tucked her in to sleep in the back of his rental car with a movie playing on his tablet to hide some of the noise.

Nikki had collapsed in relief after seeing Trevor's dead body. She grabbed Floyd's hand and cried from the bottom of her soul. Not tears of sadness, tears of hope.

As Bree finished answering questions, two detectives tried to push past Trooper Floyd to arrest Nikki. Bree rushed forward to support Nikki and did nothing to hide her suspicions.

Nikki shrunk back and gripped Bree's hand. "He's one of them," she whispered.

"I know all about Gruber. Tell me, did your husband order the corporate center to be blown up and Detective Gruber to call it accidental?"

"I don't know. It's certainly something he was capable of," Nikki whispered as Gruber approached.

"Detective Gruber. Why am I not surprised to see you

here?" Bree asked as she watched Gruber's face contort in anger.

"Get away from the suspect, Miss Simpson. Or maybe you two colluded and I'll need to arrest you, too."

Bree squeezed Nikki's hand in support as Trooper Floyd tried to push Gruber away from them. A man in a dark suit got out of an unmarked car and sauntered over. He was lithe and reminded Bree of a panther. His skin was dark as night. His muscles bunched under the expertly cut suit. But it was the narrowed eyes that made Bree think he'd pounce so quickly you'd never see it coming.

"It appears I made it just in time. I'll take over, thank you."

Gruber turned on the new arrival. "You? Who the hell do you think you are? I'm the detective around here, not you."

The man smiled, but it was a deadly smile. "Agent Delmont of the FBI. I take it you are Detective Gruber? What a happy coincidence I was able to witness you trying to arrest a victim and a bystander. It'll make my paperwork that much shorter."

"What are you blabbing about?" Gruber had gone over the edge. He poked his finger into Agent Delmont's chest and brought his face inches from Delmont's.

In a blink, Gruber screamed out as Delmont grabbed his wrist, twisted it behind his back, and slammed him into the car. "Detective Gruber, you're under arrest for assaulting a federal agent, taking bribes, criminal racketeering, and fraud."

Gruber tried to fight the handcuffs but Delmont just slammed him into the car again. Bree heard Nikki snicker. It had to be a relief to her. Tonight, two of the people who terrorized her were being brought to justice.

"Miss Simpson, ma'am, I'll be in touch to get statements." Delmont gave them a smile that transformed his face to one of caring and concern.

"Thank you," Nikki said as Trooper Floyd flagged over the EMTs to check her out.

Bree went over to where Logan stood by the sleeping Anna Beth and sagged into his embrace. "I did this. This is all my fault."

Logan stroked a hand over her hair and held her tight. "You saved her. You turned him in. You found a trooper who would arrest him and brought him here. You saved her life tonight."

"I should have turned over the evidence as soon as I got it. I was so consumed with the power struggle that I forgot true power is used to protect people who are unable to protect themselves. I failed, Logan."

"You might have had a setback, but it takes a big person to admit she was wrong and do what is right. You did that, Bree. There is no winning in a situation like this. It's so much bigger than that." Logan looked into his back seat at Anna Beth curled up with her pink teddy bear and frowned. "Or so much smaller than us. The main thing is that this little girl and her mother are safe. And now, I hope, you will be, too."

"I hope so. Nikki said she didn't know if Trevor ordered the explosion, but said he was capable of it. And Gruber was certainly on his payroll."

"Hopefully, you both have found resolution tonight. Look, Nikki is all cleaned up. I bet she'd like to see Anna Beth."

Bree looked up and saw Nikki coming out of the house in jeans and a T-shirt and carrying two bags. Her face was bruised and there were some butterfly stiches holding the deeper cuts together. She looked around and smiled as she saw Bree and Logan.

Logan opened the back door and slid his arms under Anna Beth. Slowly, as not to wake her, he pulled her out of the car. "I think you're looking for this little angel."

Nikki's face filled with pride as a single tear fell from her face. "Thank you for taking care of her. Tonight I had told Trevor we were leaving him. I should have known better. I shouldn't have stayed at all. I should have just left the first time it happened. I had been telling myself that he loved me. That he was sorry. But then he hit Anna Beth tonight . . ."

"It's never an easy thing, Nikki. But you survived," Logan said softly.

"That's right. I have a daughter to raise. She needs to know it's okay to stand up for herself. That even if everyone ignores the problems, she needs to address them head on. I'll make up for where I failed. She'll never be a victim again."

Trooper Floyd pulled his cruiser up and got out. He picked up her bags and put them in the back of his car.

"Thank you, Trooper. I'll sit in the back with Anna Beth." Nikki then turned and threw her arms around Bree. "Thank you for doing what I wasn't strong enough to do — finding someone who would listen. I owe you our lives. We're going to our lake house for the rest of the summer while I sell this monstrosity of a house. Only good memories from here on out."

Bree watched Nikki get in the car and Logan bent over to place Anna Beth next to her. He buckled her in and the child nuzzled up to her mother, her eyes never opening.

"I think it's time for me to take you home, too."

Bree climbed into the car and waited for Logan to get

in. It was going to take her a long time to forgive herself for not doing the right thing immediately. Mallory had warned her. What hurt most of all was knowing she'd let her father down by giving in to her need for revenge. It had been a hard lesson to learn, but she knew what she needed to do now. She had to focus on those who were getting stuck in the crosshairs of this fight. Marcus, her workers, their families . . . they were the innocent victims of this power struggle.

Chapter Nineteen

N oah put a pint of mint chocolate chip ice cream down in front of Bree without saying a word. Bree sighed thankfully and looked up at a nervous Noah. She'd been a bear . . . well another word that started with a *B,* all day today. She was mad at herself and was determined to feel every second of guilt she thought she deserved.

Bree's shoulders sagged as she took the first bite. "Thank you, Noah. I needed this."

"What are you working on so hard today? Is it anything I can help with?"

Bree looked down at all her notes on the domestic abuse shelter she wanted to build and shook her head. "No, this is something I need to do. Have there been any problems at the work site today?"

"Nope. All is well. Oh, you did get a call from Logan who said he was going to pick you up at six for dinner. And Elle wanted me to remind you that your final dress fitting is the day after tomorrow."

"Thank you, Noah," Bree smiled before taking another bite of ice cream. All of her sisters had a weakness for ice cream when things got tough.

Bree licked the spoon and sent Legal her plans for the charity she wanted to start. After brooding most of the night, Bree had realized she wasn't at fault and neither was Nikki—it was all on Trevor. But it still didn't make her feel better.

So far his death had managed to stay out of the papers since a minor was involved, but she knew it was only a short time before some reporter found it.

Bree only had a couple of hours until Logan came to pick her up. While the events last night had kept her up all night, Logan had kept her up for the rest of the day. He'd been her hero last night. The way he'd quietly comforted Anna Beth had warmed her heart. And if she was honest with herself, he already held a special place in her heart. She'd already known it. The trouble was making herself vulnerable by admitting she loved him. A warm feeling flowed from her when she thought of him. It was the concern she had for him. It was the way she couldn't imagine her life without him in it.

"Earth to Bree." Bree blinked and when the world come into focus she was looking at a banner that read *Sexiness Has No Age*.

"When I have a look like that on my face, it's usually because I'm reading one of *those* books." Shirley sat down and fanned herself. "Phew, even I learned a thing or two from them."

Bree just stared at Shirley as she went on talking about the books she reads. How had this come up? As Shirley continued on from cowboys to vampires, Bree felt the stress fall away. Soon she was laughing at Shirley's commentary. Sometimes all it took was a good laugh to bring clarity into your life. Yes, she still blamed herself for what happened last night. But instead of being weighed down by guilt, she was going to do something about the problem, not sit on the sidelines. And she was in love. In love with a man who would cradle a crying child, a man who flew back to Atlanta just because she was in a car accident, a man who challenged her to be a better person while supporting her to be who she is inside.

A weight lifted with each laugh as Bree admitted the feelings swirling inside her. She'd learned her lesson about power, and while she was wrong about handling Trevor, she was never going to make that mistake again. She admitted her fears of failing to herself and found she had the strength to pick herself up. She could stand up for herself, just as her father had said she could. And she admitted to herself that she loved Logan. But could she admit it to Logan?

"And when the vampires get to sucking . . . Bree are you listening to me? I'm talking about hot vampire sex here."

"I don't know about Bree, but I sure am listening." Logan grinned from where he was leaning against Bree's office door.

"Logan!" Bree and Shirley said at the same time. Bree was nervous, but the look on Shirley's face as she gave Logan a once-over had her laughing again.

"Yeah, you would make a hot vampire. Did you know they can have sex all night long?" Bree coughed and Logan just slowly grinned.

"Then maybe I'm part vampire after all," he said with a wink.

For the first time in Bree's life, she saw Shirley blush and stare at Logan completely speechless. Of course Bree was having difficulty finding her words as well. Instead, images of Logan's slate-colored eyes glowing as he nibbled her neck filled her head.

Logan stood with a smile on his face as he watched

Shirley and Bree stand there open-mouthed. He couldn't believe they hadn't heard him. He'd even knocked, but then he caught Shirley's conversation and decided to eavesdrop a little. It was always a mystery as to what women talked about, and now he knew. They talk about sex—just like men do. However, he was pretty sure he had never talked about having sex while galloping across the vast Texas plains or tucked away in a plush-lined coffin.

"Logan," Bree stuttered again. "What are you doing here?"

"It' six o'clock. I'm here to pick you up for dinner. Or we could skip dinner and try out some of the things Shirley was talking about. I might be able to dig up some silk ties . . ."

He smiled again at the sound of Shirley and Bree gulping. He had been trying to give Bree time to come to terms with their one night together. But after listening to all this talk of sex and seeing the way Bree was eyeing him, he didn't feel like giving her any more time or space. Dinner at the romantic restaurant was going to be dramatically different from what he envisioned. And was he going to have fun!

Logan walked into the room, took Bree's blazer off the back of her chair, and helped her slide it on. He turned to face her and straightened the lapels, letting his fingers brush the sides of her breasts. Bree's eyes widened and she inhaled sharply.

"Ready?" he asked, picking up her purse and holding out his arm for her to take.

Bree nodded and slipped her hand into the crook of his arm. As he escorted Bree from the room, all he heard was Shirley whispering, "Lordy!"

Logan was able to get the smallest table in the farthest corner of the family-owned Italian restaurant. He poured Bree another glass of wine and continued to rub his thumb over her knuckles. He loved her reaction to him. Her cheeks had the sexiest blush that reminded him of their one night together. With every shift of his leg, his thigh would brush against hers under the table. The way Bree was pressing her leg into his told him she was just as affected by this slow torment as he was.

His plan for tonight had been an old-fashioned wooing. He was going to take her out for a romantic dinner. Then they were going to walk under the stars where he was going to tell her how much he loved her. But after seeing the way she practically devoured him with her eyes, he decided on another tactic. He was going to show her he wasn't kidding when he said he could make love to her all night. Then when she was completely sated, he'd tell her he's in love with her. It sounded like the perfect plan to him.

Bree took another sip of wine to wet her dry mouth. Logan had been driving her crazy all night long. He'd shift in his seat and his leg would press against hers. She'd feel his muscles taut and warm next to hers. Her mouth would go dry as she remembered rubbing those bare legs with hers . . . and now he was whispering his fingers against the sensitive skin of her wrist. She was sure he felt her pulse leaping, and by the sexy smile on his face, he was enjoying every minute of it.

Damn Shirley for talking about sex for an hour. Her

whole body was nothing but a bundle of nerves now — a bundle of nerves Logan was expertly strumming.

"Are you ready to go?" Logan asked. His voice seemed rougher and lower now.

Dammit, Shirley! She was thinking about Shirley's cowboy story. Logan could definitely be a cowboy. The muscled thighs she'd been feeling all night could squeeze —

"Are you okay? You look flushed," Logan whispered as he helped her slide into her blazer.

"Um . . .y . . . yes," she stammered. Smooth, Bree, real smooth. She tried to pull away and take a deep breath. If she could only have a second to herself to gather her wits, but no, Logan kept his hand on the small of her back as he led her from the restaurant.

"There's a great view from my hotel room. I thought we could order some dessert and enjoy it." Logan's voice was so low and sexy she almost came right then. She only nodded as he drove off.

Logan made sure he kept touching Bree all the way to the hotel. A hand on her knee, a brush of his arm against hers — anything to keep her thinking about them together. He was enjoying this assault on her senses and, by the hungry look on her face, she was, too.

He had kept his desire under control, but as they neared the privacy of the elevator he could feel it starting to slip. Logan followed her into the elevator and pressed the button to the ninth floor. The second the doors closed, he was stepping in front of her and pushing her back against the wall.

"I'm done waiting, Bree. There are things we need to discuss. And we will . . . in the morning. Tonight you're mine."

He bent his head and captured her lips in a fiery kiss. Bree responded, threading her fingers through his hair. Logan pressed his body against her. His erection throbbed with need as he ran his hands over the curve of her hips.

The elevator stopped and the doors opened, but Logan paid no attention as they tugged and pulled at each other. Managing to get out of the elevator by sheer luck, Bree decided to take control. She pushed Logan against his door and began to unbutton his shirt as he fumbled with the key. The sight of her small hands on his bare chest had him shoving the door open and pulling her inside. The door slammed at the same time his shirt fell to the floor next to hers.

He never broke their kiss as he stripped Bree of her clothes. His hands moved up her ribs and cupped her breasts. They fit perfectly in his hands, and when he rolled her nipples between his fingers, she moaned into his mouth before wrapping her hand around his length, leaving him hissing out his breath.

Bree's body vibrated with excitement as Logan moved his lips down her jaw to her neck. He felt her pulse leap as he continued to kiss his way across her collarbone before he dipped his head lower and pulled a hard nipple into his mouth. He strained to control himself as Bree let out a slow moan of pleasure.

He cupped her most sensitive area and teasingly ran his finger lightly across her wet lips. She thrust her hips forward, seeking fulfillment to her growing need. Logan grinned against her breast. Bree had finally had enough teasing and pushed him back onto the bed.

"I think I've let you play long enough. It's my turn now."

Logan fell against the cool sheets and put his hands

behind his head. He watched her climb on top of him and start to explore his body, gripping the pillow to stop himself from shoving her into the mattress and taking her right this second. Instead, he clenched his jaw and let her cover his chest with light, teasing kisses. Her long hair feathered along his skin, making his muscles ripple in anticipation.

When her warm kisses moved to his erection, his whole body jerked with sexual tension.

With a growl, Logan moved his hands from behind his head and grabbed Bree by the shoulders. She didn't even try to hide her smile as he lifted her up and flipped her onto the bed. He covered her body with his and reached for the condoms he had bought.

"I'll get that for you," Bree said with the look of a tigress about to go in for the kill. She grabbed the condom from his hand and slowly slid it over him, her fingers teasing him as she went.

"All's fair in love and war, sweetheart," Logan got out through his clenched teeth. "And I intend to win this battle and have you screaming my name so often you won't have a voice by morning."

"I'd just like to see you try," Bree shot back with a smile that made his erection jump in her hand.

Without saying a word, Logan bent his head and captured her lips in a fierce kiss as he plunged two fingers into her. When he had her panting, he removed his fingers and slid into her in one strong thrust. Just as he knew from the first time with Bree, she wasn't a bystander to sex. She wrapped her legs around his waist and met each stroke with one of her own. Her nails dug into his shoulder as they both pushed each other toward pleasure. She was fighting him for control and what an enjoyable battle it was. As she screamed his name, he shouted hers.

Chapter Twenty

Bree fell against the pillows and watched Logan climb from the bed. She enjoyed the view of his perfect behind as he headed to the bathroom. She rolled over and looked at the clock. It was already three in the morning. Time flies when you're having hot sex. Apparently you become oblivious to everything around you, too. Thunder clapped and lightning lit up the room.

Bree swung her tired legs off the bed and took a couple of shaky steps to look out at the massive storm. She'd loved watching storms all her life. The way the thunder drummed and the rain played music on the rooftops soothed her.

She pulled aside the sheer curtain and peered out into the night. Lightning flashed and the skeleton of her building was illuminated. Bree smiled at it. A sense of pride filled her. This was hers and it was coming along. She had reason to believe it would be done in time and become a beautiful addition to downtown Atlanta. Lightning burst in the sky again, and Bree suddenly narrowed her eyes. She saw a man at her construction site, the person responsible for all the sabotage. She couldn't see him clearly from this far away, though.

Bree sprinted for the door only to skid to a stop to grab Logan's shirt and pick up her heels. "I got him, Logan!" Bree screamed before flinging the door open and shooting

173

out into the hall. She ran past the elevator as she buttoned the shirt. She slammed her hands into the metal bar of the stairwell door and ran headlong down the stairs. Her bare feet slapped at the concrete, but she didn't care. All she could think about was getting there in time to find out who was causing all this trouble and pain.

She pushed the bottom door open and sprinted through the luxurious lobby as the night crew stared after her. The rain soaked her in seconds, but the lightning lit her way. Her bare feet splashed through the rainwater on the street as she ran across it to the construction site. Cursing that she didn't have her boots, Bree struggled to slip the high heels onto her wet feet. As soon as she got them on, she felt a nail lodge in the sole of her shoes and was glad she had at least some protection. Bree ignored the nails and debris and darted into the shadows of the construction site on her tiptoes.

Logan heard Bree shout but couldn't understand what she said while he washed his face. He set down the washcloth and opened the door to the bathroom. "What did you say, Bree?"

Logan patted his face dry with a towel and slowly lowered it from his face as he realized the room was quiet, too quiet.

"Bree?"

Logan peered around the empty room puzzled. Her dress was still there, but her heels were gone. Her purse still lay by the door. It was then he saw the drapes to the window open. He hurried to the window and looked out at the corporate center in time to see Bree darting across the street.

Logan didn't waste time. He shoved his legs into his

pants and gave up looking for his shirt. He found one shoe and slid his foot into it as he frantically looked for the other one. Valuable time was passing. It felt like forever, when in reality it only took him a couple of seconds to locate the other shoe.

He bolted from the door and hoped he wasn't too late to protect her from whatever danger was lurking in the storm.

Bree's heels sunk quietly into the mud forming around the build. She slowed her pace and lifted her foot from the mud as she pressed herself against the newly arrived crates of building materials. Her foot hit something hard and she held her breath, hoping the man didn't hear it. She could catch glimpses of him as he moved around the interior of the building. He had grown bold and turned on a flashlight as he moved.

Bree looked down at what she had hit and picked up the metal crowbar. It couldn't hurt to have this with her. She snuck forward with the crowbar laying flat against her naked leg. She didn't care, though. She didn't care that the dark blue dress shirt was clinging to her and barely covered her bottom. All she cared about was finding out who this man was.

She stepped out of the rain and into the building. Floors and ceilings had been repaired and were keeping the worst of the weather out. Bree went up on her tiptoes as she quietly made her way toward the last place she saw the light. The sound of feet scuffing the ground caused her to spin around and peer into the darkness. Bree gripped the crowbar tightly against her leg and frantically scanned the shadows. Her heart beat loudly, and she forced herself to take slow, deep breaths. Everything looked sinister.

The impact was so sudden that Bree didn't have time to react. She went down hard on the concrete and was quickly flipped onto her back as a weight settled across her hips. She looked into the black mask where the face of the man straddling her should have been.

"So you are watching me like I am watching you. I thought you'd get my message and come meet me. Nice outfit." His voice was a harsh whisper that Bree struggled to hear against the storm.

"According to your letters, you like my outfits. I'm glad I didn't disappoint."

She felt rather than heard the man chuckle. "It's a shame things weren't different. Together we'd have no limits—no one getting in our way. We'd take over Atlanta together. But, alas, it cannot be."

"Why can't it be?" Bree asked as she slowly moved her fingers along the concrete in search of the crowbar she'd dropped when she was hit.

"Don't play dumb. I know you're not, so knock it off," he hissed, agitated at her. Bree's middle finger felt something hard and cold. She flinched at his words and managed to move her arm just enough to palm the crowbar.

"You're right. I'm not," she said as she closed her hand around the crowbar and swung at the same time Logan spotted them.

"Bree!"

The crowbar met with the man's shoulder. He grunted and ripped it from her hands. "Three's a crowd. Next time we meet, we'll be uninterrupted."

The man pulled back his fist and Bree covered her face with her arms to protect her face from the hit. Instead, she felt all the air rush from her lungs as his fist connected with her solar plexus. She gasped for air and rolled to her side.

The pain of having the wind knocked out left her struggling as she watched the man disappear into the night.

"Bree!" This time Logan was next to her, running his hands over her, looking for injuries. "Are you okay? Where are you hurt?" Bree tried to gasp for air but panic clawed at her.

"Can't. Breathe."

She felt Logan's arm slipping under her shoulders and pulling her up. "Here. You got the wind knocked out of you. Sit up and take deep breaths."

Bree sat up straight and struggled against the panic. She continued to gasp but soon she was breathing normally again.

"What happened?"

Bree let her head fall back against his shoulder as breathing became easy once again. "When you called out, he punched me in the stomach and ran away."

"What happened before that? Who was he?"

"I don't know. He had a mask on. But he said he's been watching me and knew I would come."

Headlights filled the construction site with light as people started to rush to them.

"Freeze!"

Bree looked up at the young police officer with a mop of unruly blond hair trying to stay contained under his hat. "I'm Bree Simpson. I own this building. And this is Logan Ward. He's the architect," Bree said as loud as she could. It still hurt to raise her voice after the punch.

"Let me see some identification," the officer said as he kept the gun trained on them and stepped closer.

Logan shifted behind her and pulled out his wallet. "Here's mine. Bree saw an intruder from my hotel room and rushed out without her purse. She confronted a man in a mask who then assaulted her with a punch to the stomach as I came upon them."

"Is this true, ma'am?"

"Yes. He knocked the wind out of me and ran off in that direction," Bree pointed to the last location she'd seen the man.

"Stay here, please," the officer said as he took off in the same direction.

"You may want to go with him. He's a baby," Bree said as she struggled to stand.

"He's old enough to be a police officer, sweetheart. I'm sure he'll be fine. But you are not so lucky."

"What do you mean?"

"What the hell were you thinking about taking off alone and mostly naked?"

Bree felt herself stiffen at the criticism. "Excuse me?" she asked quietly. What right did he have to berate her? "You're acting as if you have a say in what I do."

"Oh, Bree, stop it. I know you're tough. I know you feel you must stand up to bullies. But you don't have to be strong all the time. I'm here, too, you know."

"For a week!" Bree was embarrassed when her voice cracked with emotion. This was the real reason she'd been acting tough. She was alone. She didn't have anyone to be her partner in life. She didn't have anyone to stand behind her supporting her. She cleared her throat and tried to stop the tears pressing against her eyelids. "You're only here a week, Logan. I can't depend on you. If I start and you leave . . ."

"Oh, sweetheart," Logan said softly as he pulled her into his arms and rested his chin on the top of her wet hair. "Can't you tell I love you?"

Bree's heart swelled and then plummeted into her

stomach. "I love you, too. But, Logan, what are we going to do?"

"I don't know. Whatever it is, we'll do it together."

The sound of a throat clearing had Logan turning quickly and shielding Bree from potential harm. Instead, it was just the young officer standing there looking uncomfortable.

"I'm sorry to interrupt. I found fresh footsteps in the mud, but the rain washed them away pretty quickly. I snapped a picture, but that won't help too much. Do you think you need an ambulance, Miss Simpson?"

"No, thank you. I'm fine now, Officer . . ." Bree said as she peeked around Logan's wide shoulders.

"Macey," the young man supplied. "If you'd like, I have a blanket in my cruiser. I'll bring it in here and take your statement."

"That's nice of you, Officer Macey, but I won't waste your time. All the reports I've filed have all ended in the garbage anyway."

"What reports?"

"The explosion, the cut locks, the destruction of equipment. I just got my car back from when it was vandalized. But nothing was ever done about it. Gruber made sure of that. So don't worry about a little assault," Bree said with a smile. She wasn't mad. She'd stopped being mad after Gruber had been arrested. It was just the way it was.

Officer Macey's lips thinned in a hard line as he shook his head. "Oh no, Miss Simpson. I won't let anything happen to you or your property. Gruber is a disgrace to the uniform. He's not the only one either, but ninety-nine percent of us are the good guys. I'm going to prove it to you."

Bree watched Macey stalk out to the car and come back with a tablet and a blanket. "Let's start at the beginning. When was the first act of vandalism?"

Bree looked in surprise at Logan who just smiled. "It looks like we have some help after all. Officer Macey, get ready for a long night."

The three of them sat on upturned buckets as Bree and Logan told Officer Macey of every incident since she'd been awarded the contract.

Logan finished up the questions Officer Macey had for them as the first rays of light streamed through the steel beams of the corporate center. Bree had fallen asleep an hour ago. This certainly wasn't the way he wanted to spend their morning, but Officer Macey had decided to champion them.

"You know, there's an Agent Delmont with the FBI who's heading up the investigation into Gruber. You should contact him with any information."

Bree stirred in his arms as a ray of light hit her face. She tried to shove it away but finally gave up and cracked her eye open.

"Morning," he said, dropping a kiss on her head as Officer Macey looked slightly embarrassed.

"I'm so sorry I fell asleep."

"It's all right. Mr. Ward answered all my questions and Miss Weston sent me the video footage. Unfortunately, we didn't see a face or a car, but at least it's something to go on. I will not let you down. I'll get to the bottom of this. Don't you worry, Miss Simpson."

Logan smiled at his earnestness and helped Bree stand

up. He quickly pulled the blanket around her to hide the wide span of legs she was flashing.

"Thank you, Officer. You're right. Just a few bad apples can spoil the bushel. I should know better than to give up hope. You've restored that for me. Please keep me updated on anything you find."

"Oh, I will. You can count on me!" Officer Macey hurried to his cruiser and took off.

By the time Bree and Logan had walked half-dressed through the lobby of the hotel and talked the front desk into giving them a new key, she was ready to crawl into bed for the rest of the day.

"Come on, let me run a hot shower for you, and then you need to get some sleep." Logan led her into his room and turned on the shower. It seemed an eternity since they had been making love, when it really had just been a couple hours.

"I'd better call Noah and tell him I'm taking this morning off and tomorrow afternoon for my dress fitting," Bree groaned, "and I have to call my family."

"You call Noah and I'll fill your family in on what's going on while you take your shower."

Bree let out a sigh of relief. She loved her family, but she was starting to feel as if she had nothing but horrible news to tell them. This week should be all about Elle and Drake, not her getting into trouble. Her mother would kidnap her and lock her in the house if things didn't get better soon.

"Thank you. And please reassure Elle I will be there for the fitting tomorrow afternoon." Bree shuffled her feet for a minute. Last night had been scary and lovely all at the same time, but it seemed unreal. She had to know for sure.

"Logan?"

"Hmm?" Logan mumbled as he looked around for his cell phone.

"Did you mean it? Do you really love me?"

Logan stopped looking for his phone and came to where she stood in the middle of the room. His pants were starting to dry and his bare chest was warm as he held her in his arms. He stepped back and tilted her chin up so she could look in his eyes.

"I do. I love you very much, Bree. I think I started falling for you when I saw you in that pink hard hat from my window. I love the tough woman you show the world, but I love the vulnerable softy you are under that shell just as much."

"Oh, Logan. I love you, too. It takes a strong man to stand up to me without trying to push me down. Your support and love . . ." Bree sniffled and then smiled up at him. For the first time, she was not worrying about when he was leaving. "Well, it makes me fall even more in love with you."

Logan leaned down and kissed her. It wasn't like the kisses from last night. In this slow, deep kiss she could taste his love. His hands drifted from where he cupped her face, down her shoulders, over her spine to where the blanket was wrapped around her waist. She felt a gentle tug and the blanket fell to the floor.

"I believe my shower is waiting," Bree said as she pulled away. She stepped back and gave him a slow smile as she unbuttoned the shirt she borrowed from him. Bree slid the shirt from her shoulders and dropped it on the floor. With a wink, she sauntered into the bathroom, giving him a perfect view of her swaying behind. Bree disappeared into the steamy shower. She heard the curtain open behind her and smiled to herself. Logan hadn't kept her waiting.

Chapter Twenty-One

Bree made her way down the empty corridors without paying attention to where she was going. Her mind was on Logan. She had ended up calling Noah yesterday morning after her shower with Logan and telling him she was going to be working from home. She and Logan had slept well into the afternoon.

After waking up, they both worked in comfortable silence until dinner. It had been nice spending the day together. He worked on a new design and she answered emails. She'd even placed a bid on a new project in Macon, Georgia. She found it very nice with Logan there. She watched him while she talked on the phone and discovered he cracked his knuckles as he thought about design aspects. Little things like that made her feel as if she were seeing a side of him no one else had.

After they were caught up on work, Logan had taken her home where she'd dressed in jeans and tennis shoes. She'd packed a bag of food and they'd had a picnic dinner at Centennial Olympic Park. They had laughed, told dirty jokes they'd learned on construction sites, and talked about their dreams. The world had fallen away around them until they were the last two people on the planet.

This morning she had woken in Logan's arms to a ringing phone. Real life was intruding. However, when she found out the call was about Marcus being able to go home, she leapt from bed, kissed Logan, and hurried to the rehab facility.

Bree turned down another beige corridor and stopped in front of Marcus's room. He was standing by his bed talking to his therapist and looking as if nothing had happened to him. Bree almost broke down in tears.

"Your ride is here," the therapist said with a smile as she nodded to Bree. "Enjoy being home, Marcus. I'll see you tomorrow for therapy."

Bree waited until the young woman left before rushing over to Marcus. "You look fantastic. Oh, Marcus, I'm so happy for you!"

"I should thank you. This prosthetic is top of the line and makes it easier to get used to."

"Well, come on, let's get you home," Bree said with a grin that filled her whole face. She was bouncing with energy as she watched Marcus slowly make his way toward her before sitting in his wheelchair.

"Not perfect, but it's getting there. Thanks to you and your family." Marcus's smile faded and Bree worried that he was thinking of the explosion.

"Nonsense. I think it was because of that hot little therapist. Is she the one you were telling me about?"

"Yes. She won't date any patients, though," Marcus said sadly as they stopped in the lobby. Marcus used a crutch and stood up. Slowly, Bree walked with him to the car just outside the door. He was starting to sweat with the effort and looked a little pained.

"Are you okay?" she asked while unlocking the car.

"Yes. I have to work on my stamina. You know amputees have run marathons and climbed mountains. I'm not going to let this stop me from living my life. Then I'll be able to ask her out on a date. Oh, you got your car back!"

Bree laughed and got in the car. "Finally! I know Reid loves me, but I'm afraid he'll never let me borrow another car since I wrecked his last one."

Marcus turned somber. "You didn't wreck that car. Someone tried to hurt you. No, someone *did* hurt you. It never should have happened. They went too far."

"Marcus, I'm fine. And I have great news. Detective Gruber was arrested by the FBI." Bree told him of Trevor, Agent Delmont, and Officer Macey. "It's all coming around. It'll be fine."

"And Logan? You've mentioned his name quite a bit," Marcus prompted.

Bree blushed as she pulled into Marcus's neighborhood. "We're together. Though he has to leave in a couple days to go back to London. His boss only let him have a week of vacation."

Marcus started to look nervous and kept his head turned as he looked out the window.

"Nervous about coming home?" Bree asked as she turned into his street.

"Bree, there's something I need to tell you. I've been putting it off, but . . . Whose car is that?" Marcus asked hesitantly as Bree stopped in front of his house.

"My mom's. She came here early and cleaned the house. She also stocked the fridge. If you're lucky, she may have made you some dinner and a pie," Bree smiled at him as she jumped out of the car.

Marcus opened the door and used his crutch to steady himself as he slowly stood up. "I don't know what to say. Y'all have been too kind. So much more than I . . . Look, Bree, I've been trying to tell you . . ."

"Welcome home!" Margaret called as she flung open

the front door. "I've got it from here, Bree. You'd better hurry to your dress fitting."

"Oh gosh, I almost forgot. I'm sorry to dash off on you, Marcus. Call me if you need anything. I'll stop by and talk after the wedding. I'll bring pictures and cake," Bree leaned forward and kissed his cheek.

"Okay. It can wait. And, Bree . . . thank you. You're the best person I know and you don't deserve what's happened to you."

Bree smiled and rolled her eyes playfully. "That speech gets you two pieces of cake." Bree waved as her mother expertly fussed over Marcus.

"Allegra! What? Did you think I was one of your size 00 models?" Bree tried to screech, but it came out in short breaths since the pale yellow bridesmaid dress was so small it was cutting off her oxygen.

Elle snickered as Allegra hurried over and fussed with the dress. "It still looks good on you — even if it flattens your boobs and shoves them up to your chin."

"I'm sorry. You missed when I took measurements so I just snagged a dress from your closet at Mom's house."

"From Mom's? Those were from high school! You know she never throws anything out." Bree took quick short breaths and hoped she didn't pass out.

"Then you should have given me your measurements the five times I asked," Allegra shot back.

Elle and Mallory just laughed as Allegra started tugging the zipper hidden along her side. With a whoosh of air, Bree's lungs could finally expand when the zipper was down.

"Okay, enough laughing," Elle said as she still giggled. "Can you fix it, Allegra? We do kind of need Bree there, considering she's the maid of honor."

Allegra shook her head. "It's too small. I'll have to make a new one overnight. Even if I let this one out, she'd need a corset or something just to be able to breathe."

"Oh, Leggy, I'm sorry," Bree said seriously. She hardly ever used her little sister's childhood nickname, but she felt just as bad as she had when she'd broken the head off Allegra's doll when she was six years old.

"It's okay." Allegra let out a long sigh. "It's not like I have anything else to do at night. Now stand still and let me get your measurements."

"Come on, you can't lie to us. I see you texting all the time. And then that stopped when you and Finn started, um, *working* together," Elle pried.

Allegra blushed and the girls all laughed. "Leggy, you and Finn? Really?" Bree asked before being stuck by a pin. "Ow!"

"No. Finn and I aren't together."

"She didn't say she didn't want to be together," Mallory pointed out with a sly smile.

Bree laughed and was rewarded with another pinprick. Her poor sister wasn't used to teasing. Allegra was always the perfect one, the sweet one, the never-in-trouble one. Bree was the opposite. She'd been the one who always messed up, always got into trouble, always pushed the boundaries . . . and she was proud to say she still did.

Finally settling back on her knees, Allegra looked up from her notepad. "Okay. I've got you all measured. I'll get to work on this tonight and have it finished by the rehearsal dinner tomorrow night."

Bree leaned down and gave her sister a kiss on the

head. "Thanks, sis."

Elle pulled out her cell phone and turned it on. "Here's the schedule. Make sure you got this," . . . *cough, cough* . . . "Bree."

"Ha-ha." Bree rolled her eyes as she grabbed her phone to add the times to her calendar.

"Tomorrow night we meet at the church at five. Dinner afterward at our house. Then Saturday at one, we meet at the spa for lunch and pampering. Then we head to the church at five to get dressed and have a light snack before the ceremony at seven-thirty. After pictures, we drive to the Art Museum where Drake and I met for the reception. Got it?"

"Yes, ma'am," Bree teased as she got dressed.

Elle raised a brow and then smiled slowly. "I take it Logan will be joining us?"

Allegra and Mallory took the bait and soon Bree was very sorry for teasing her sisters.

Logan sat at the desk in his hotel and watched the workers over at Bree's building. She had been right. Adding workers and eating the bonus she'd get for being ahead of schedule would allow her to meet the milestone. Too bad he wouldn't be around to see it. He stared at the email from his secretary telling him Mr. Clarke expected him back at work on Monday morning.

A knock at his door pulled him from his thoughts. He answered and hid his shock at seeing Drake in his doorway.

"I hope I'm not interrupting anything," Drake said as he stepped into the room.

"Not at all. Just sending some adjusted plans back to

London. What can I help you with?"

"Elle's worried. And when Elle's worried, I become worried."

"Is she okay? Did something happen?" Logan asked as he waited for Drake to take a seat.

"She's worried about her sister. She's worried you'll leave and Bree will be left alone with a broken heart. Now, I hate all this gooey talk. But if you get married, you'll soon discover you'll do about anything to make your wife feel better. So here I am."

Logan shifted uncomfortably in his chair and looked out the window. He didn't say anything. He couldn't. He didn't know what to say. He loved her. He didn't want to leave, but his livelihood was in London.

"Did you design these?"

"Hmm?" Logan looked back to see Drake flipping through the notepad of houses he'd designed.

"Oh. Yes, but it's just a hobby. I love thinking of people in my houses. How they would use them, what would make their lives easier. I've designed a couple houses that rely heavily on technology — voice commands and so on."

"Now this I can talk about," Drake said as he leaned forward. "I've been working with Reid to integrate a new system into the resort he's building. Everything you need at the touch of your fingers."

"I thought you were a smartphone guy?"

"I am, but I'm also a software guy and this is all software. Tell me more about this system you've thought of."

Chapter Twenty-Two

The streets of Atlanta were full of people heading home from work. The sound of animated conversations made the town feel alive. It helped Logan think about his conversation with Drake. He loved the movement of the city and getting a glimpse into the lives of people in their own separate worlds. It helped him relax.

Mr. Clarke had called his residential designs ridiculous. Clarke Group did not design little houses. They designed monuments to business success. But he felt excitement when he worked on houses and projects that could make a difference in a person's life.

After Drake explained the kind of technology he was developing for Reid, the two had started brainstorming on how to integrate it into everyday life.

"You should start you own architectural company," Drake had told him. "Then we could partner on the technology aspect."

Drake's words had been stuck in his head ever since. His own company? Could he take a leap like that? He'd seen the pressure it put on his family—the way legacy meant everything. And he hated the idea of treating a company as if it were a mandatory sentence for the whole family. He saw what the money and pressure to always be the biggest, most respected company did to a family. It made them forget about their children. He was treated like an employee before he could even talk. He was the company's future.

But Drake had his own company and he didn't act like that. And the Simpsons had a company one hundred times larger than Ward Stone and Brick. They were still a loving family. Bree had told him how her father started the company and brought Shirley along. Then when he died, she told how the siblings had grown the company. And she allowed them to do whatever they wanted — whatever they *loved*.

What did Logan love? He loved houses and Bree. If he started his own company, if he took that risk, then he could stay in Atlanta with Bree. Could he really have everything he loved?

"Holy shit. Logan?"

Logan stopped walking and blinked. He'd been so lost in thought he hadn't realized he had just walked right past his own brother. "Bradley? What are you doing here?"

"I was going to ask you the same thing. I just left a meeting at Simpson Global. I met with the big shot."

Logan looked up and saw his thoughts had led him right to Simpson Global's offices.

"Elle?" Logan asked automatically. Wasn't she doing wedding stuff?

Brad's brow furrowed as he looked Logan over. "Since when do you know about business stuff? And no, I met with her brother." Brad's chest puffed with pride. "He wants Ward Stone for a resort he's building. We're negotiating price. I'm playing it hard. They have the money. We're going to make a killing off this sale. So, what are you doing here?"

"I'm the architect on the corporate center headed up by Simpson Global," Logan admitted somewhat hesitantly.

"Ah, I've dealt with Noah before," Brad said. "He's B. Simpson's right-hand man. Now, there's someone you don't mess around with. That brother is hard core, so you better not jack up the price too much. I couldn't believe it! I added twenty percent onto our price and Mr. Simpson, Reid, that is, didn't even bat an eye. He just handed it to some old woman, who I swear is old enough to have seen Atlanta burn during the Civil War, and told me he'd get back to me soon."

Logan was suddenly embarrassed. Shirley had been there and Shirley knew about his family. He wished he hadn't said anything to her. But he also didn't want to see the Simpsons get screwed.

"I don't think that was a wise idea. Why would you mark it up like that?"

Brad looked at him like he was an idiot. "Because, they have more money than they know what to do with. They have a long history with us. They trust us and they'll just pay it. I'll even come back and offer them a five percent loyalty discount. So, what are you doing tonight? Stacy and the kids are here—Mom and Dad, too. They'll want to see you."

"I have plans tonight and I head back to London on Sunday."

"What about tomorrow? Or Saturday?"

"Tomorrow I'm attending a large dinner party and Saturday I have a wedding to go to." Logan hoped his brother wouldn't push. There was no way he was going to meet up with his family. Not after hearing Brad talk like that. It soured his burgeoning dream of running his own company.

"Everyone must be getting married that day. Reid said his sister is getting married this weekend, too. Well, there's a simple solution; just cancel your dinner for tonight," Brad said in his haughtiest voice. Brad and their father never thought twice about breaking an appointment. It made them feel important.

"Logan?"

Oh no. He felt the panic rise as he heard Bree's voice behind him. His brother looked her over appreciatively and Logan had a strong desire to knock him out. Strange, he had been angry when he found Stacy in his brother's bed, but nothing compared to what he was feeling now.

"Sorry to interrupt, but I got the strangest text from Shirley about—"

"Bree! This is my brother, Bradley Ward," Logan said, cutting off whatever Bree was about to say. The last thing he wanted to do was let Brad think he had an "in" at Simpson Global. He and his father would try to exploit it for all it was worth.

Brad held out his hand and smiled. "You can call me Brad. It's nice to meet you, *Bree*," he said, emphasizing her name. "So this is why you're so busy. Mom and Dad would love to meet any woman of yours. Stacy was beginning to think you'd never get over her. I must say, this is a relief!"

Logan felt Bree stiffen next to him. During their date at the park, he'd told Bree about his family and their company. Of course she'd know about their company, having handled all the negotiations in the past with them. And he'd told her about Stacy. He just didn't tell her it was Brad's bed he'd found her in. He felt her suddenly relax and she batted her eyes. Her lips formed what Logan could only describe as a ditzy smile.

"Oh, darling! You want me to meet your parents?"

Again she batted her lashes up at Logan and the spark in her eyes had him trying hard to keep a straight face. This was the mischievous Bree her family had told him horror stories about. Somehow, though, it made him feel young and free and equally mischief.

"But, honey bunny, I thought you wanted a romantic dinner again. Just like we had the other night."

Bree blushed right on cue. Brad was enthralled. "I don't know if I can handle another night like that," she whispered before giggling.

Logan smiled. Sadly, he'd dated women like this and watching Bree in character made him happy she wasn't really like this. She was real. She was intelligent and liked debate on subjects more important than which country club was the most exclusive. She was B. Simpson and Bree all in one amazing package.

"Hold on, it's Stacy," Brad said as he pulled out his cell phone. "Hello, honey. You wouldn't believe who I am standing here with."

Logan leaned down and whispered into Bree's ear. "I really don't want to do this."

"Because someone didn't tell me his fiancée cheated on him with his own brother! How could you leave that part out?"

"It's embarrassing. I thought you'd think less of me."

"Oh, Logan, I could never think less of you."

Brad laughed and Bree and Logan looked up at him. "Yes, honey, I'll insist they join us. Love you, too." Brad hung up the phone and Logan thought Brad looked as if he were in on some joke that he and Bree weren't.

"Stacy was with Mom and Dad. You know how much they just love her. Anyway, they absolutely insisted you and *Bree* come to dinner with us tonight. We have reservations at Beau Monde. It is *the* restaurant in Atlanta."

Bree clapped her fingertips together and gushed, "Oh, the Beau Monde! We just have to go, honey bunny!"

"Wonderful!" Brad said triumphantly. "We will meet you there at eight tonight."

Logan watched his brother walk away and suddenly the game felt a little too real. "We aren't actually going, are we?"

Bree just laughed. "Of course. I haven't had this much fun since I put a stink bomb in the cheerleaders' dressing room."

"He doesn't know you're a Simpson. And he made the same mistake I did. He thinks B. Simpson is a man."

"Then this is even better. How could he do that to you? How could a guy steal his own brother's fiancée? He deserves payback. I wonder if I can find another stink bomb before dinner?"

"I told you about my family. About the pressure to be in the family business, to be the head of society in Charleston . . . it is all about appearances. Emotion never factored in. They're nothing like your family. Nothing."

Bree took his hand in hers and gave it a little squeeze. "You have us now. I know we are not a substitute for your family, but maybe if you tell your parents how you feel, they'll back off a little and see that you are happy at your chosen profession."

Logan bent his head and kissed her. "Thank you for being so supportive."

"I've heard that's what girlfriends are supposed to be like," Bree teased.

Logan kissed her again. He liked the sound of her being his girlfriend. But when he thought of Bree, he didn't think of her as his girlfriend. When he thought of Bree, he thought of her as something more — his partner in life, his love, his heart, and his future wife.

Bree melted against Logan right there in the middle of the sidewalk. She didn't care if her whole office saw them kissing. Meeting his family would help her understand him a little better and maybe, just maybe, she could help him start mending some fences.

"Just what the hell are you trying to pull? I should beat the crap out of you, Logan," Reid said through gritted teeth as he ripped Logan and Bree apart.

"Reid!"

"Stay out of this, Bree. This man is using you and playing us." Bree stepped back without thinking. She'd never seen her brother so furious.

"What are you talking about, Reid?" Logan was clearly as confused as she was.

"Sending your brother in here to fleece us, that's what. If you think I'm going to pay this exorbitant fee just because you and my sister are . . . are . . . you know, you are wrong."

Logan held up his hands and shook his head. "I have nothing to do with my family's company. My brother has no idea I'm dating your sister. He only thinks I'm the architect for *Mister* B. Simpson."

Bree nodded and placed her hand in Logan's. "It's true. Besides, Logan didn't even know I had a meeting with Mr. Ward today. Actually, I didn't either. I had Noah rearrange my schedule since I was at my dress fitting."

Reid was starting to look convinced. "So, Noah called me to handle this because it's my project and Logan is what, estranged from his family? Why?"

"Yes, and that's Logan's business," Bree answered.

Reid just looked at Logan and raised an eyebrow.

"It's okay. It doesn't seem as important anymore," Logan said to her. "I don't approve of the emphasis my family puts on their social standing. That, and I found my fiancée in bed with my brother."

Reid's anger faded from his face. "That's horrible. I'm sorry. Sometimes I forget not everyone has a family like we do."

"It would have been a dream come true to have a family like yours," Logan told him.

"You do now," Reid said as he slapped Logan on the back. Bree couldn't love her brother any more than she did at this moment. "We'll see you tomorrow for the rehearsal. Hope you don't mind that I'm going to lay into your brother for pulling this crap."

"I think B. Simpson may take care of it," Bree said seriously.

"Damn. Now I kind of feel bad for him," Reid teased before heading back into the office building.

Logan laughed but quickly grew worried. "Bree, you know I'm nothing like my brother. I don't want anything from you. I have money of my own. I have an occupation of my own. I have interests of my own. I just want to share it all with you."

Bree's heart swelled. She did know that and it was freeing. "I do, Logan. And I love you even more for it. But now, *Bree* needs to get ready for dinner tonight. On the way to the restaurant, I'll tell you what Allegra did to me. Or rather what I did to her. Oh, and I better call Jean Blanc and tell him to pretend not to know me."

"Who is Jean Blanc?"

"He's the owner of Beau Monde. He always makes a table available for me. I love French food — well, mostly the desserts. I can't eat snails. I always picture them as what

Reid would stick on me when we were playing. I can't imaging actually eating the slimly little guys."

"Reid used to stick snails on you?" Logan asked, trying not to laugh.

"Yep. But I got him back. I put a snake in his underwear drawer. He screamed like a girl and refused to wear underwear because he was too scared to open the drawer after that," Bree said proudly.

"How did you get the snake in his drawer?"

"It was just a corn snake. They're fairly tolerant of people and hardly ever bite if you're gentle with them. I knew there were a few by an abandoned house just down the street from us, and I brought one home. After it ate, I just picked it up and put it in the drawer. It was happy and content to curl up and sleep with a full belly . . . until the screaming started. My dad made me take it back to the old house as my mom stood guard with a shovel just in case it decided it wanted to live at our house."

"That's priceless. You'll need that spunk to handle my family tonight. I really do wish you had said no. I don't know what they'll do or say."

"It's okay. I'll handle it. I'll even put on my big girl panties tonight."

"No panties would be better."

"Who said my big girl panties were anything other than metaphorical?" With a wink, Bree got back into her car and drove home to get dressed.

Chapter Twenty-Three

L ogan held Bree's hand tightly as he walked into the upscale French restaurant. Bree had tried to keep him entertained with the story of her fitting that afternoon, but he was too nervous to fully enjoy it. For the first time, he wasn't really worried about seeing Stacy and Brad together. No, he was happy things hadn't worked out with her because now he had Bree and he loved her more every day he was with her.

What he was worried about was if Bree would still love him after meeting his pretentious father and brother. Would she still love him as his father repeatedly spoke on how disappointing Logan was and how superior Brad is? And would she still love him when his parents berated her "lineage" as if she were a brood mare.

"Bonjour, étranger!" a little man with a huge smile called out.

"Bonjour," Logan replied stiffly. Why was the man calling them strangers? But then the man and Bree shared a wink and Logan realized he'd just met the owner.

"You speak French, monsieur?"

"Oui. I spend a lot of time in France for business. Beautiful countryside and I could stay in the mountains forever." Logan relaxed a little as Jean Blanc radiated happiness.

"Oh, Mademoiselle Bree, he is, how you say, a keeper." Jean winked as a waiter came forward.

"This is a beautiful restaurant. You must be very proud," Logan told him. The man puffed with pride.

"*Oui!* It is my heart. I am happy every day I come to work. It makes it no longer work, yes?" Jean smiled as Logan nodded. "Ah, table twenty-eight please," he told the waiter.

Logan's mind started spinning. Drake had said something similar about his job. And when he and Drake had brainstormed, it hadn't felt like work at all. It had been fun. He felt energized and couldn't wait to do more. He didn't feel like that at Clarke. For all the pomp and circumstance his father insisted on, his father truly loved his work. Brad did not. Brad loved money.

Bree squeezed his hand again and stood slightly nervous by his side when they stopped at the table. The dress she wore had the table staring at her and he couldn't blame them. It was a deep-green silk halter dress that flowed down her body. It showed off her rather favorable assets on top and tightened around her small waist before flowing down to her knees. The tantalizing glimpse of cleavage was highlighted with a gold chain that wrapped around her neck and formed a *V* down her chest.

"Hello Mother, Father," Logan said rigidly.

"Did you forget about me already?" Stacy purred in the voice she knew he used to like.

Looking at her now, he wondered what he ever saw in her. She was a beautiful woman. Tall and willowy, but her brown hair had been turned to blonde. Her B cups had been enhanced to Ds, and her slightly large nose was now narrow with a slight upturn at the end. She was fake — simply molded to fit Brad's vision of the perfect wife.

"This is Stacy? The Stacy you used to be engaged to?" Bree asked, slightly shocked.

"So you've heard of me?" Stacy asked, pleased.

"Well, sure. We laugh about it all the time." Stacy's smile fell to a sneer. "And Brad," Bree cooed. "It's so nice to see you again."

Stacy's eyes went so wide the end of her fake lashes came unglued. Logan coughed to hide his laugh. "Bree, these are my parents, Carolyn and Charles Ward."

"It's such a pleasure to meet y'all. You must be very proud to have raised a son as wonderful as Logan," she said with such honesty that Logan wanted to kiss her right then and there. Instead, he raised her hand to his lips and placed a kiss on her knuckles.

Her father cleared his throat as Logan held out a chair for Bree and then took his place next to her, placing a protective arm over the back of the chair.

"We would be if—" his father started before Bree stared her father down.

"Yes, we are," his mother finished. Bree relaxed and started talking to his mother about Charleston as the first course was served.

"Just what exactly did you tell her about us, Logan? Obviously, you are spewing lies since you aren't over us. How many times do I have to tell you—I love Brad, not you," Stacy hissed.

This time it didn't even bother him. "I only told her the truth. And trust me, you have nothing to worry about in regards to my feelings. I stopped loving you a long time ago—the second I found you in bed with my brother, in fact. A person who does something like that isn't worth the time or energy to love. Bree, on the other hand, I love very much."

Logan turned in his chair to listen to Bree and his mother talking animatedly about the historic sites around Charleston. His mother sat to Bree's left and he let his thumb trace over her bare back as he listened to them talk. He'd never seen his mother so enthusiastic. He knew she was on the Historical Board, but he thought it was for name only. Clearly, he was wrong. His mother and Bree shared a passion for history.

He looked across at his father and saw that he was just as amazed. "Why, Carolyn, I had no idea you loved history so much."

"Oh yes, right along with my roses," Carolyn said happily.

"Don't tell me you're one of those people who can actually get things to grow?" Bree asked in mock amazement, but it was enough to draw his normally timid mother into a thirty-minute discussion on gardening. She was also president of the garden club. He enjoyed watching his mom blossom under Bree's confidence. She seemed to feed off of it, and he loved seeing it.

After the main course was cleared, it appeared his father had had enough talking about history and flowers. He smiled indulgently at his wife but then jumped in as soon as he could to change the subject.

"So, Bree, how long have you and my son been together?" he asked. Stacy and Brad stopped whispering feverishly and turned to listen. The interrogation was about to begin.

"Oh gosh, not that long. Almost three weeks, or is it four? After the explosion—and that seems like a lifetime ago," Bree laughed.

Everyone else at the table froze. "Excuse me, did you say explosion?" his father asked in disbelief.

"Yes, your son saved my life and the life of a friend of mine. We were in a building and there was an explosion. Logan ran through fire to find us. He and another man lifted a steel beam off my friend. My friend ended up losing his leg, but not his life, thanks to Logan and Al. And when Al went to carry my friend out, Logan stayed behind and looked for me. He found me not far away and carried me out of the building through a wall of fire. Your son is my hero."

She looked up at him with such love Logan kissed her again right there in front of his family. "I love you," he whispered against her lips.

"I love you, too."

"Oh my goodness, that's so romantic. My son, the hero! I'm so proud of you, Logan," his mother said, reaching across the table to pat his hand. Even his father seemed temporarily impressed.

Bree smiled at Logan. He was her hero and she was proud of the strong man he was. He looked out for those in trouble, even if he didn't know them. He was a good man, a man she wanted to spend the rest of her life with . . . if only he wasn't leaving again in a couple days.

"So, what do you do, Bree?" Charles asked, stopping her thoughts from going too far into the future.

"I work in construction," she answered vaguely.

Stacy snorted. "Your girlfriend is a construction worker. Priceless."

Bree really didn't like Stacy. While it was clear Logan could care less about her, Bree felt she needed to show Stacy what she had missed out on. Logan didn't deserve to be treated like that.

"I didn't say that, did I?" Bree asked sweetly. "I'm more

on the business side. But I can certainly use a hammer if needed. After all, I am sure the Wards didn't get to be where they are today without putting a few bricks together. You have to get your hands dirty to learn a profession."

"Good point. I learned to make bricks from my father and his father before him. I taught Logan, but Brad never did learn," Charles told her. "But who are your people? We have to look out for our son. He can't be involved with a nobody. Our family is one of the oldest and most prominent in all of Charleston."

Bree didn't know if she should be shocked, insulted, or just laugh. But she'd experienced this her whole life. Instead of being insulted, she just shrugged her shoulders.

"I work with my family," she answered without giving away who her family was. Under the table, she squeezed Logan's knee to let him know she was all right and then finished answering as vaguely as possible. "We've lived in Atlanta for three generations. Before that, my family were farmers in Scotland. My great-great-grandmother was known to be a very good weaver."

"A weaver? Your family was a bunch of peasants?" Stacy asked incredulously.

"Yes. Like most people who came to America for a fresh start. I am sure the Wards have a similar story."

"They were laborers in England," Logan told Stacy. "Everyone starts from somewhere and it's nothing to be ashamed of. Dad loves the rags-to-riches story of the Wards."

His father grunted. "The point Stacy is making is she's a nobody now. While I admire her family trying to build themselves up, they haven't done it in the three generations they've been here. You have to know that we are the targets of scams because of our wealth."

Bree sucked in some air. Logan started to open his mouth, but Bree squeezed his leg to tell him to shut up. "You're so right, Mr. Ward. You have to be careful of women who hop from one bed to another just hoping to get pregnant to secure their financial well-being. But I can assure you I don't care about your money or your position in society."

Logan didn't bother hiding his laugh this time. Stacy radiated anger and even his parents looked at her with new eyes.

"Well, I'm glad we got that out of the way," Bree said happily. "So, Brad, what were you doing downtown this afternoon?"

Bree kept her innocent smile on her face as she led a bragging Brad blindly down the path of his own destruction. B. Simpson was about to have her say.

"Well done, son," Charles said after Brad told them about his meeting with Reid. "Too bad B. Simpson wasn't there. I hate that we have to wait to hear back from them. He was always a tough one, but we'll come out ahead of this battle."

"I'm sorry to interrupt, but do you really think it's a good business model to jeopardize someone's trust just to try to scrape out a few extra dollars?"

"Bree, I don't expect you to understand how this works, but it's how we made our fortune — the one you're hoping to get your hands on."

"Charles!" Carolyn snapped. "Apologize. She has done nothing to earn that remark."

"Don't worry about it, Mrs. Ward. I have thick skin," Bree said nicely. She really did like his mother. Now the rest of the family was something different. "Excuse me for a moment. I'm going to go freshen up before coffee."

Bree stood up and gave Logan a smile and walked as calmly to the bathroom as she could. Once out of sight, she deviated to the kitchen and out the back door so she could scream for all she was worth. Letting out a deep breath, she pulled out her cell phone and called Reid.

"How far are you from Beau Monde?"

"Five minutes, why?"

"I need you to do me a favor. Remember in high school when you helped me stand up to Missy Shoemaker for spreading all those rumors about me?"

"Yeah."

"Well, I'm at dinner with Logan's family. His mother is a sweetheart, but his father just accused me of being a golddigger and his brother is bragging about taking Simpson Global for a tidy gain."

"They would do that with you at the table?" Reid asked outraged.

"They don't know who I am. Remember, they think B. Simpson is a man. All of my previous negotiations were done in writing or through Noah. I don't have time to negotiate every deal."

"Oh, sis, that's mean. They just opened their mouth and inserted foot, huh? I'll be there in five."

Bree took another deep breath and hurried back inside.

"Bree?"

"Mrs. Ward! What are you doing?" Bree asked as she made her way through the kitchen. The staff all knew her and thought nothing of her being back there. They all just nodded and said hello in French.

"I was looking for you. Oh, Bree. I am so sorry. Logan has always followed his own path. Right now he's widening that path that led him away from his family by giving a well-deserved tongue-lashing to Charles and Brad.

I hope you understand my concern. I was so hoping to bring Logan closer again, and now I fear he'll be even more alienated."

"I don't think your husband understands Logan's principles."

"I don't think he does either. They've never seen eye to eye and Charles has always been too focused on turning Logan into his image instead of encouraging him to find himself. But Logan has found himself, and done it without his father's support. I'm proud of him for finding a job he loves and a woman he obviously cares for. Please accept my apology."

"I do. I just don't accept your husband's and Brad's since they never offered one. So, I'm sorry to say, they're just going to have to learn their lesson." Bree patted Carolyn's hand and walked back to the table.

Logan stood as soon as Bree returned with his mother hurrying behind her. "Let's go, Bree."

"It's okay. I want to give your father and brother a chance to apologize for judging me without knowing me."

Bree sat down and didn't look up at Logan. Instead, she stared down his father and brother who just stared right back. Logan had told them what he thought about them when Bree left. He even lit into Stacy, but it didn't make him feel any better. It was a relief to get his feelings off his chest, but he found he didn't care if he had their approval anymore.

"Ah, here they are," Jean Blanc said happily with Reid trailing after him.

Logan shot a look to Bree as she simply looked up at Reid and smiled. What was she up to? Whatever it was, he was about to find out.

"Ah, Mr. Simpson," Brad said as he stood up and shook Reid's hand.

"Sorry to interrupt, but B. just called and discussed the contract. I figured you'd want to know Simpson Global's answer right away."

"Of course! Let me introduce you to my family. This is my wife, Stacy, my mother, Carolyn, my father and president of Ward Stone and Brick, Charles Ward."

Logan enjoyed the fact he wasn't introduced as part of the family. He looked at Bree again, but she wasn't giving anything away.

"Mr. Ward, ladies. It's a pleasure to meet you all. But, I'm kind of surprised; I didn't know you already knew B."

Brad looked confused and Logan bit the inside of his cheek to keep from laughing. Considering that he went through this same thing, he should have sympathy, but he didn't.

"I'm sorry, but we've never met Mr. Simpson. We've only negotiated through email and through calls with his assistant," Brad told Reid.

"Funny guys. Anyway, I guess you wanted me here to help with the facts of the meeting, so I'll summarize. I met with Brad today to purchase limestone for the out-building by the lake at the resort. He put the price at $300 per ton, which is way above market value. Why don't you take it away, B.?"

"This isn't funny, Mr. Simpson," Charles cut in before Bree could answer. "I don't know what kind of joke you think you're playing, but we don't know Mr. Simpson. I thought you were here to talk business."

"No," Bree said finally standing up and walking over to her brother. *"We're* here to talk business. I hadn't wanted to bring it up over such a lovely dinner. Since dinner was anything but lovely, except for dear Carolyn, that is, there was no reason to delay our business dealings."

"What are you talking about?" Brad challenged.

"You wanted to know B.'s response, so here she is. She can tell you herself," Reid said as he stood shoulder to shoulder with his sister.

Logan couldn't hide the smile anymore. The looks of utter confusion on the faces of his family were just too much. He laughed even harder knowing he'd had that same look on his face when he realized the woman he had quickly started having feelings for after the explosion was the same person he thought was the devil, continually changing the design of the corporate center.

"Let me clear some things up. I'm Logan's girlfriend, Bree Simpson. I'm also the V.P. of Simpson Steel and Construction, and I am rejecting your outlandish bid for stone and will stop all future orders. Gentlemen, you've lost my business. Carolyn, you are welcome at my home anytime. Now we can go, Logan."

"With pleasure." Logan stood and tossed his napkin on the table. "Oh, and I'm quitting Clarke Group and starting my own architectural firm here in Atlanta."

"That is great. I bet Elle and Drake will be your first clients. They've been talking about finding someone to design a house for them," Reid said happily as he led the group outside.

"Oh, that's wonderful, Logan!" Bree said, genuinely happy for him. "I'm so happy for you, but leaving London?"

"I love you, Bree. I'd do anything to be with you. But this is ultimately about me. It's my passion. Designing and building houses is what I long for. I want to be my own boss. And of course, Atlanta is where I can have that and you."

"Okay, I'm out. I don't need to see this mushy stuff." Reid shook Logan's hand and gave Bree a kiss on the cheek before heading out of the restaurant.

"I couldn't leave you again," Logan cupped her face with his hands and looked into the eyes of his future.

"I was looking into moving to London," Bree confessed. "Now take me home, Logan. Quickly."

"I think I can manage that. But it will be the last thing I do quickly tonight."

Chapter Twenty-Four

"Where's Mallory?" Bree whispered to Allegra as they got in position for the rehearsal.

"She got called away on business. Cousin Mary is standing in." Mary walked down the aisle in front of them at the wedding planner's cue.

"Isn't that strange? She missed the shower and now the rehearsal?"

Allegra shrugged as she watched Mary walk slowly toward the altar. "I do, but what can be done? Elle doesn't seem too upset. She said it goes hand in hand with Mallory's job."

"Please. I think something happened between Mallory and Reid. Haven't you ever noticed they're never in the same place together? Something is up."

Allegra started walking slowly down the aisle on cue, but looked back at Bree quickly. "Mallory and Reid have always been very different. They might just not like each other and want to spare putting us in the middle."

Bree thought about that as she watched her sister walk down the aisle. Maybe, but it sure would be interesting to see them together at the wedding tomorrow.

Logan sat at the large rectangular table at Drake and Elle's house and laughed. Everyone there was smiling and teasing one another. Reid, Bree, and Allegra were trying their hardest to embarrass Elle with childhood stories and warning Drake of her particular quirks. This was what family was supposed to be like.

Shirley thumped the table with her glass and brought his attention back to the conversation at hand. "No, no, no. The reason we had separate twin beds back then wasn't because we didn't have sex. Come on, most people had four or five kids. Think about it. You didn't really watch much television and once it got dark, there wasn't much to do, so we had a lot of sex. Without those twin beds, we'd never get any sleep!"

"Ew, come on, Shirley. I don't want to think about that," Reid joked.

"You just don't want to admit you're not the Casanova you think you are. Now, Cary Grant, he was a Casanova. They don't make men like that anymore."

"Or Paul Newman," Margaret called from the kitchen.

"I always loved Clint Eastwood. Now that is a man." Drake's mom sighed as the ladies all giggled.

"Okay, enough of that. Did Logan tell you his big news yet?" Reid asked.

Logan felt all eyes turn to him. Margaret and Drake's mother even popped out of the kitchen and quickly glanced at Bree's left hand. "News? What is it, dear?"

"Well, Drake really should be included in this, too. He's the one who planted the idea in my head. I've decided to move to Atlanta and start my own architectural firm."

"That's wonderful news," Elle said excitedly. "Drake and I just moved into this beautiful house, but it doesn't feel like it's *ours*. We have found the most perfect lot. We were thinking of building a house next spring and we need an architect. Do you think you could build our dream house for us?"

"Please," Drake added. "I saw some of your designs and they're amazing. Plus I think we may be working together on a business project as well."

"I'd be happy to have you two as my first clients." Logan shook Drake's hand and soon the table was full of conversation about the house and his new firm.

Bree basked in the happiness around her. Everyone was laughing and the dangers of the past month seemed so far away. More importantly, she'd found a love like her parents had—the same kind Elle and Drake had found. She had been prepared to leave Atlanta if she needed to. But seeing how Logan fit so perfectly into her family and how they could all give him the love and support he deserved, she was glad he decided to move here. One day, maybe he'd be designing a house for her to build for their own family.

"Okay, Bree. It's time to try on your dress," Allegra told her as she walked back inside carrying a large garment bag.

"I think that's my cue to leave," Reid joked. "Logan, you said you needed to stop by the hotel to check out. Do you want me to take you?"

"That would be great, thanks." Logan gave Bree a quick kiss and stood up. "You'll be okay getting home?"

"Of course. I have two of Mallory's men in the driveway. I'll be fine. I'll see you at home." Bree loved the way that sounded. Home . . . with Logan.

Bree watched them leave, then headed upstairs with Allegra and Elle to try on her new dress. Allegra pulled it out of the bag and held it up.

"Wow. I can't believe you made this whole thing in a

day. You are beyond talented," Bree told her sister.

Allegra blushed and looked slightly embarrassed. "Thanks. Here, try it on."

Bree slid into the dress and Allegra zipped it up. It fit perfectly.

"I'm going to have the hottest bridesmaids ever! You look amazing in that dress, Bree." Elle clapped as Bree did a little spin. The dress had a sleeveless, form-fitting top that flowed into a full-length A-line gown. The pale yellow looked romantic and made Bree glow.

"And the shoes . . ." Allegra looked around. "Oh, no. I left them at my apartment!"

"I'll get them tomorrow. Don't worry about it," Bree said as she tried to calm her sister.

"No, I really need to see you in the dress with your shoes so I can make sure the length of the gown is right. I can meet you at home in thirty minutes. I'll bring the shoes and it will take just a second."

"You'd better not argue with her. You know what a perfectionist our little sister is," Elle teased.

"Really, Allegra. The dress is perfect, but if you want I'll meet you at my house."

"Thank you. I really would feel much better if we did that."

Bree and Allegra kissed Elle goodnight and hurried to their cars. The men Mallory hired turned on their car and the procession headed out the gates. Bree drove slowly and watched every oncoming car. Her security guards had said they would drive, but Bree was fighting for control of her life. She wasn't going to give in to fear and allow whoever was behind this to take her freedom from her.

Her street was quiet as she pulled into her driveway.

She waited for the garage to open and one of the guards to search it and her house. When he came out the kitchen door and gave her the thumbs-up, she drove into the garage, lowered the door, and headed inside.

The guard had turned on the lights for her and she set her keys on the kitchen counter. She turned on the television and looked at the clock. Logan would be arriving soon. She dug around her junk drawer and pulled out a spare key. Bree had never given a man a key to her house before.

"Crap. The dress."

Bree set the key down and hurried to her car. She lifted the trunk and pulled out the dress her sister had worked so hard on. There was a small sound, then a pinch on her back before she heard the zap of a taser. Her muscles tensed and she fell to the floor, gripping the soft yellow dress as the world turned black.

Logan waved to the security guards as he pulled into Bree's driveway. This was the first time he was going to walk inside and say, "Honey, I'm home!" It was the beginning of the rest of their lives. This weekend was Elle and Drake's, but he had already snuck away to ask Drake which jeweler he used.

Grabbing his bags from the backseat, Logan walked up to the front door. He set one bag down and turned the handle. Locked. He rang the doorbell and waited. Nothing. He looked in the window and knocked. The sound of a car pulling into the drive made him turn around.

"Hey! So sorry to interrupt your first night together," Allegra paused, "well, not together . . . I mean, I'm sure you've been together . . . together as roommates. No, wait that's not right."

Logan just laughed. His future sister-in-law was so flustered he decided to have mercy on her. "I know what you mean. I just got here. She must be upstairs because she's not answering the bell."

"Is she home?" Allegra asked, coming up the steps with a shoebox in one hand and a massive sewing kit in the other.

"The lights are on, and her security is right there across the street."

"She's probably taking a shower. Ring the bell a few more times while I take a peek in the back to see if she left the door open."

Allegra handed him her things and hurried around the side of the house.

"Is everything okay, sir?" a guard asked from his place in the car.

"Bree didn't leave, did she?"

"No, sir. She got home about fifteen minutes ago. Why?"

"She's not answering the door. She's probably taking a shower."

The front door opened and when Logan turned around he knew it was bad. Allegra stood there, her face white. "She's not here, Logan. The side door to the garage was unlocked."

"What?" Logan pushed into the house as Allegra frantically waved for security. He searched the house from top to bottom. Her car was there. Her keys were on the counter right next to a spare key meant for him.

"What should we do?" Allegra asked him. He didn't know. He had to find her, but where?

"We found tire marks. It looks like someone came through the side door and took Bree out the back. There are drag marks in the grass through a neighbor's yard, and they stop at the curb the next block over," one of the security guards told them.

"I've alerted Mallory who has called Agent Delmont and Officer Macey. She's on her way over here now," the other said as he rushed from the upstairs. "Nothing seems out of place."

"Oh, Logan, what's happened to her?" Allegra cried. Logan put his arm around her and wrapped her in a hug.

"I don't know, but I'll find her."

"Don't tell Elle or Mom! They can't know. Not right now. This is one of the happiest times for them."

Allegra was right. They'd wait until the last moment to bring them in if they needed to. Hopefully, they weren't far behind whoever took Bree.

The front door flew open and Mallory stormed in. She was all in black. Black-heeled boots, tight black jeans, and a black top that hugged her bombshell body. Her long, wavy blonde hair hung down her back. She looked like a menacing angel.

"Update!" she demanded.

The guards hurried to fill her in as she looked around.

"Here's what we're doing. Damien and Delmont are heading to some of Jeff's known locations. Officer Macey is checking on Trevor's properties. I have men checking on Trevor's wife, just in case she became upset with Bree. I'm covering every base I can think of."

"I'll call Finn. He can help," Allegra suggested, already sending a text.

"Good. When he gets here, you two go to Simpson Global and make sure they didn't take her there. I've already alerted security there," Mallory told them.

"I have men heading to various construction sites belonging not only to Trevor and Jeff, but also some of her other competitors."

"What about the corporate center?" Logan asked.

"I'm going to go there," Mallory replied.

"Not without me."

"Then let's go."

Bree was exhausted. Her muscles ached and she had a severe case of cotton mouth. Slowly, she tried to wet her mouth only to find she couldn't. A strip of cloth was actually stuffed in her mouth. Her eyes shot open and she stared into the darkness of a construction site. She was sitting on a metal folding chair. Her hands were tied together, palm to palm, in front of her. Her chest was also bound to the chair and her legs were tied to the chair legs.

Moving awkwardly, she pulled the cloth from her mouth and gasped for air. Oh no! The cloth that bound her hands and had been stuffed in her mouth was a beautiful pale yellow. As her heart slowed, she heard the sound of the freight elevator rising.

Looking around, she took in the walls and design of the building she was in. She was on the top floor of an unfinished building. The ceiling above her was not yet complete and she could see the sky above. She could yell, but she didn't think it would do any good. This high up in the city, the sound would bounce and it would be impossible for a bystander to know where it was coming from—if they even heard her.

No, she had to think her way out of this. She started

looking for something she could use if she got free. And she needed to find an exit. She saw two flights of stairs, one in front of her and one behind her where the freight elevator was about to open. Sometimes this high up in a new build, the only thing available was scaffolding, covered in netting to stop anything from falling below and hurting people. But it could at least get her down a floor.

She continued looking and saw a table saw, a welding machine, and a cooler with *Al* written on it. Bree stopped and her eyes flew back to the cooler. This was *her* building. In the blink of an eye, she was imagining the last plans of the building from every angle. There was scaffolding on every side of the building from the top beam above her down to the floor below her. And, if she was really desperate, there was the debris chute. The trouble was getting there.

She tested her bonds again and they gave a little. A little was all she needed. With older siblings, it wasn't as if she hadn't been tied up before, and Reid and Elle were much better at knots than this person. Taking in a deep breath, she leaned forward as far as she could. Bree hooked her thumbs under the strip of Allegra's beautiful dress and then exhaled all of the air from her lungs. It was enough to move the chest strap up and over her breasts. She slouched and wiggled in the chair until she worked the strap up and over her shoulders. Once her shoulders were free, she was able to simply lift the strap over her head.

Dumbasses, they should have tied her hands behind her back. Bree grinned in victory as the sound of them coming out of the stairwell grew louder. Bending quickly, she started to untie her legs. She got one undone and was about to get the other when the elevator door opened into the room and two voices became clear.

"I'm telling you, I'll have no part of this."

Bree froze. She knew that voice.

"And I'm telling you, you owe me too much to back out now." She knew that voice, too. No! It couldn't be. The betrayal cut so hard she fought for breath.

"I fulfilled my obligation. Call your men and tell them to leave my mother alone."

"You fulfill your obligation when I say you do and not a moment before."

Bree heard the men coming closer. Should she run? Could she leave him, even after betraying her? It was clear he was being extorted.

"Stop. You've hurt her enough. You asked me to spy on her. You asked me to delay the plans. I did that. Now live up to your end of the bargain and let my mother go."

Bree sat still and waited for them to come. She placed her leg back in place and hoped if she sat still long enough, they wouldn't notice she'd gotten most of the way free. As much as the treachery hurt, she understood it.

"You almost killed us! I lost my leg. Isn't that enough?"

"Not until she's dead. And you're going to do it, Marcus."

"Jeff," Bree said with her most authoritative voice. "I believe Marcus can go. This is between you and me."

The men behind her froze. "Bree, I'm so sorry!" Marcus yelled before she heard Jeff punch him.

"Stop!" Bree shouted as Jeff dragged a limping Marcus in front of her. He had to be in pain. His face was deadly white and his whole shirt was covered in sweat. Even if they used the service elevator, he wouldn't be used to so much activity. She didn't know how he'd managed. That's when she saw the blood seeping through the knee of his tan pants.

"Do you know the rule for never getting caught? Never do your own dirty work," Jeff pulled a gun out and placed it to the back of Marcus's head.

Bree felt anger building inside her. Marcus was trembling, and his leg was going to give out on him. Jeff was exploiting them both. Playing on their emotions for his own gain.

"Why, Jeff? Why go through all this trouble?" Bree asked.

"Simple. Money. This job should have been mine anyway. But you with your little skirts and big tits had all the owners panting. It was lucky a friend of my uncle's is part owner. He tried to get me the job, but everyone wanted the *next big thing* — you." Jeff laughed. "At least I got him to add the language that if you didn't meet your milestone you were out, and I would be a shoo-in."

"You don't want to kill me, Jeff. You could have done that numerous times already." Bree tried to keep him talking as she noticed Marcus grow weaker and weaker.

"Deep down, I respect you. You're a tough broad. I never wanted to kill you. I just wanted to disgrace you. But it's come to this. You're too close to meeting your goal after you poached all my workers. Now Trevor's former workers are flooding to you begging for jobs."

"And Marcus?"

"I had to, Bree. Jeff found out I went to summer camp with Mr. Clarke's son and he has my mother," Marcus's voice was uneven and his breathing was ragged.

Jeff just laughed. "I don't really have her. She's just being watched. If she were to have an accident down in Tampa, then that would be most unfortunate. There would be no way to connect it to me, just like your unfortunate murder won't have anything to do with me. Marcus, go pick up that piece of rebar."

"No. I won't do it," Marcus said as forcefully as he could.

"Then not only will you die, but your mother will, too . . . right after she learns of your death. It will break her heart to hear her little boy killed his boss in a jealous rage and then killed himself. No one will question a man spending so much time with a woman and not falling for her. That's why there aren't many women on construction sites. Then it won't be very hard for me to just toss you off the side of this building."

"It's okay, Marcus. Do it. Get the rebar."

Chapter Twenty-Five

Mallory floored her black Porsche 911 Carrera and Logan held on. They hadn't said a word. As she shot down the interstate at over 120 miles per hour, he figured talking wasn't really the best idea. He didn't know why, but he felt Bree had to be at her construction site. It was where that man had lured her before. It had to mean something, but what?

Mallory entered the exit ramp, barely slowing down. She weaved her way around traffic as the buildings of downtown grew closer. Logan could feel the tension coming off of Mallory as she ran a red light. She was a contradiction if he'd ever seen one. Normally the epitome of a Southern belle, tonight she looked flat-out deadly. There was a lot going on under those long lashes and red lipstick.

"Do you know how to use a gun?" she asked as they neared the construction site.

"I was state champ for skeet shooting," Logan told her as he stared up at the dark building.

"Good. There's a shotgun in the trunk. You take that one. I'll take the others." She turned off the lights and stopped at the coffee shop next door. Without saying a word, she got out of the car and opened the trunk. Inside the tiny trunk were a shotgun and a metal case.

Mallory handed him the shotgun and popped the barrel

open to load it. She pulled out the case and opened it. She selected a handgun and tucked it into her back. Then she pulled out two knives and slid them into her stiletto boots.

"You're a very interesting person," Logan said as they moved into the shadows of the building.

"You have no idea."

Bree begged Marcus to move. She gave him an encouraging nod, but he shook his head. "No. I can't kill you."

"I rather have it be at your hand than Jeff's. Please, Marcus."

"Listen to the lady, Marcus."

"Marcus," Bree said when it was clear he wasn't going to move. "Someone has to look out for your mother. She's old, alone, and you're all she has left. Please, at least you can be with her and live. There's no reason for three of us to die tonight. And you know he'll kill us all if you don't do it."

Bree stared at Marcus and silently begged him to move. With a defeated exhale, Marcus took an agonizing step toward the rebar. His knee buckled and he fell hard to the floor.

As soon as Marcus hit the ground, Bree made her move. She leapt forward and swung her leg in a high sweeping kick as hard as she could. The tie held and the force of her kick sent the chair arching through the air behind her leg. Her foot hit the gun in Jeff's hand, and the chair knocked him to the floor before crashing back into her.

"Bree, run!" Marcus panted from the floor.

Bree ignored him as she bent to untie her foot. Jeff scrambled up and started for her.

"I hate for it to be this way, but a man's gotta do what a man's gotta do."

The hit came hard and fast. Bree screamed and the punch connected with her stomach just as it had the other night. She stumbled back and the chair clattered along the floor as she struggled to stay upright.

Logan followed behind Mallory as they darted into the first floor of the corporate center. As soon as they saw the two cars, they knew they had the right spot. Logan and Mallory stopped in the lobby and looked around. There were two staircases.

"We can't risk the elevator. You take that one," Mallory whispered. The scream that reverberated around them stopped Logan's heart.

"Bree," they whispered. Logan didn't pay attention to Mallory's last command as he took off at a dead run. He hit the stairs and didn't slow down. Stair after stair, floor after floor . . . he couldn't be too late. He couldn't lose her after just finding her.

Bree dragged in a deep breath. Her scream had emptied her lungs and she'd been able to absorb the punch this time. But Jeff was already moving on toward Marcus.

"It'll take more than that, Jeff!"

Jeff turned and looked at her. Then he looked to where Marcus was close to passing out from pain. She saw the moment he decided she was more of a threat. Bree had gotten into scraps before and she was tough. She wouldn't give up now. She had three lives depending on it. She wasn't going to go down without a fight. Bree yanked the binding from her leg and jumped to her feet.

Bree tested her bound hands again, but she didn't have time to get them out. Jeff was stalking toward her too quickly.

"Run, Bree. Save yourself," Marcus called out. She saw him struggle to get up, but when he put weight on the prosthetic, his eyes rolled into the back of his head and he collapsed in a heap.

Bree ran all right—right at Jeff. She lowered her shoulders at the last minute and dove for his knees. They both tumbled to the floor with Bree on top of his lower body. Jeff rolled out from under her and let loose with a kick that landed on her shoulder.

They both scrambled back and leapt to their feet. "I guess I'm going to have to get my hands dirty this time. All this could have been avoided if you just backed down when I gave you a chance." Jeff held a small piece of rebar in his hands and shrugged.

"I never back down."

Bree felt her breathing slow. Her focus was solely on Jeff. The rest of the world faded away until it was just the two of them. She heard her heart beating, strong and steady, and she knew without a doubt she was going to fight until her last breath.

She saw the moment he pulled back the rebar and swung. Bree waited, watching the rebar arch toward her in slow motion. She ducked at the last second, felt the breeze of the rebar passing over her head, and then leapt up. With her fingers pointing in front of her, she jabbed them into Jeff's eye. He howled in pain and dropped the rebar to clutch his eye.

Bree was relentless. She moved forward and smashed the top of her forehead into the bridge of Jeff's nose. A satisfying *crunch* was followed by a gush of blood. Jeff fell to his knees, screaming as he clutched his face in his hands.

Anger filled her as she laced her fingers together and stood over Jeff. He took advantage of people. He hurt them for his own gain. He was going to kill her, Marcus, and Marcus's mother all for money. She laced her fingers tightly together, forming a tight fist, and raised it above her head.

She wasn't going to let him get away with it.

She arched her back and used momentum and all the power she had to slam her elbow into the base of Jeff's skull. Instantly, he crumbled to the floor, unconscious at her feet.

"Bree!"

The shouting broke through her fog and she saw both Logan and Mallory running toward her from opposite stairwells with guns in hand.

"Oh God, Bree! Are you okay? Are you hurt?" Logan slid to a stop and started running his hands over her body as he took in her blood-covered clothes.

"Who is it?" Mallory asked as she hurried over to the body lying at Bree's feet.

"It's Jeff."

"Is he alive?" Mallory pressed her fingers to his neck. "Yep. You did a hell of a job on him," Mallory said proudly as she made her way to check on Marcus. "What's Marcus doing here?"

"Call an ambulance. Oh, Marcus!" Bree pulled herself from Logan's embrace and rushed to Mallory's side.

Logan pulled out his phone and made the call while she and Mallory turned Marcus over and tried to get him to wake up.

"Jeff extorted Marcus to spy on me and delay the build. He's the one who kept sending the demands to your boss, Logan. He knew Mr. Clarke's son, so when he called Mr.

Clarke, it didn't raise any suspicions. Then Jeff wanted Marcus to kill me to guarantee Marcus wouldn't talk. But Marcus wouldn't do it. I had to finally convince him. But I saw how much pain he was in. I knew his leg was going to give out. He took a step and down he went. That's when I jumped Jeff."

"I did a full background on him. There's nothing to extort him with. Trust me, I looked," Mallory said as she pulled a knife from her boot and cut the cloth at Bree's wrist. "Uh-oh. That fabric looks familiar."

"I know. I'm a dead woman. Since Jeff didn't kill me, Allegra surely will." Bree sighed as the soft yellow fabric stained with blood fell to the ground. "Jeff threatened to have Marcus's mother killed if he didn't cooperate. Marcus thought he was just going to get me fired from the job. He didn't know about all the violence that would follow."

Mallory bent down and used the knife to cut away Marcus's pant leg. They all gasped at the site of the amputation. Blood had soaked through the sleeve and the whole part of his leg was swollen to twice its normal size.

"I don't know how he even stood for a minute. Are you going to press charges?" Mallory asked.

"For what?" Bree asked innocently. "This man tried to save my life."

Logan slipped his arm around her and kissed her forehead as he tucked her into his shoulder. "That's my girl. I knew you'd choose the right path."

Logan kept Bree wrapped in his arms the whole time the police questioned them. Mallory had conveniently returned their weapons to the trunk of her car as she notified the authorities before calling Allegra and Finn.

Bree answered all of Officer Macey's questions and made sure Marcus left in the ambulance right away. Agent Delmont had quickly made a call to the Tampa office and heard back within thirty minutes that two men had been arrested outside Mrs. Phillips's house. They were currently being held on gun charges, but he was sure they'd flip as soon as they found out Jeff was in custody.

"Let me through! Oh, Bree!" Allegra cried as she pushed through a line of officers collecting evidence.

"Officer Macey," Bree whispered harshly. "If you appreciate anything I've done to help solve this case, then you have to do one thing for me."

"Of course," the young officer said gravely.

"Hide the evidence bags with the yellow cloth or my sister is going to lose it right here and there may be no survivors."

"Her? She looks so sweet."

"Oh, she is . . . most of the time. But like all quiet, meek, sweet people, when she loses it, she goes off the deep end. If she sees the dress she stayed up for twenty-four hours *remaking* is now torn to shreds . . . it would be bad, very bad."

The officer's face blanched as he hurriedly grabbed the evidence bags and shoved them in his jacket pockets just as Allegra reached them.

"Oh thank goodness! Are you all right? Are you injured?" Allegra pulled Bree from Logan's arms and enveloped her in a tight hug.

"I'm okay. Thank you so much. I'm so sorry this happened tonight." Bree gave a shaky smile.

"As long as you're safe, that's all that matters. We'll load up on caffeine and get pampered in a couple hours.

Elle and Mom don't have to know that you almost died right before the wedding."

Bree laughed. "So are you glad I'm alive or glad the wedding won't be disrupted?"

"Both!" Allegra laughed in return. She wobbled slightly and Finn shot out a hand to steady her. "Sorry. I've been awake for . . . I don't know, what time is it?"

"It's two in the morning." Finn smiled down at her and pulled her closer to him for support.

"Forty-four hours then," Allegra said with a shaky smile. "I don't think I could take any more. I would lose it, just lose it."

Officer Macey's eyes grew large, and Bree tried not to have her own nervous breakdown. She was so screwed.

"Finn, do you mind taking Allegra home?" Bree asked. "We're going to be here a while longer answering questions."

"Really, I'm so glad you're safe. You're my hero and I don't know what I'd do if I lost you." Allegra sniffled and everyone sucked in a worried breath.

Allegra tossed her arms around Bree again and a large sob erupted. All the men froze in place with the deer-in-the-headlights look on their faces. All except Finn, who gently pried her from Bree and held her in his arms, his dark, chiseled face showing a concerned softness.

"It's okay, Allegra. Let me take you home." Finn tucked her under his broad shoulder. Her sister looked so tiny as he tried to get her to leave.

"Thanks. I'll see you at breakfast at eight." Allegra turned to leave and then froze. "What's that yellow thing in the evidence bag?"

Oh shit. Bree was busted and Allegra was set to go ballistic. Officer Macey leapt from where he was standing and stood in front of the evidence bag near where Bree had been tied up. It was the strip she'd untied from her one leg. "Oh, this? Just some duck tape used to tie Miss Simpson up."

"Yellow duck tape?" Allegra asked suspiciously.

Officer Macey nodded his head. "Sure. Comes in all colors now and is perfect for tying people to chairs. After all, if you can't duck it, then fu—"

"Thank you for that," Bree jumped in. "It hurt like the dickens when I pulled it off. Good night, dear. I'll see you in a couple hours."

Finn got the hint and pulled Allegra away and toward the elevator. Everyone heaved a collective sigh of relief as Allegra and Finn disappeared behind the doors.

"Officer Macey, you're my hero tonight," Bree joked. "But what am I supposed to do about a dress?"

"Seriously?" Logan asked. "You were almost killed and you're worried about a dress?"

"Yes," she and Mallory said at the same time.

"Elle may not show it, but she's gone through a lot to find true love, and I'm not going to ruin it. I'm simply going to say Jeff was apprehended and everything is perfect for her perfect day. Except I don't have a dress."

Mallory grimaced. "Actually you do."

"Oh no! That thing is way too small. My breasts were shoved up so much, they were suffocating me."

Logan and Officer Macey exchanged a look that said that wouldn't necessarily be a bad thing, and Bree rolled her eyes at them.

"We could let it out as much as possible and then get you some Spanx or something to suck it all in and you'd be fine. Logan will stand nearby with an oxygen tank . . ."

"Thanks, Mallory. You're a true friend," Bree said

sarcastically. "Unfortunately, I see no other way. They tore my dress to shreds in order to tie and gag me. The only trouble is finding someone who can sew as well as Allegra." Bree snapped her fingers. "I know!"

Chapter Twenty-Six

Bree stood next to Logan as she rang the doorbell to the funky warehouse condo. Logan seemed unsure as he looked around in the predawn light. Three floors up, a light turned on. Bree rang the bell again and a sleepy voice came over the intercom.

"Hello?"

"Hi. This is Bree Simpson, Allegra's sister. I need some help."

"Of course! Come up," a second voice said a second before the buzzer to the lobby door sounded.

Bree and Logan hurried up the stairs and were met in the hall by two men with sloppy hair. "Thank you so much. I know we haven't met in person, but I'm Bree and this is Logan Ward."

The more serious-looking man with the dark brown hair held out his hand. "I'm David Bell." Turning to the energetic man with the mop of blond hair, "and this is my partner, Josh Rose. What is the emergency?"

"Is Allegra okay?" Josh asked as he practically bounced with energy even this early in the morning.

"She is, but I'll be dead if I don't get some help." Bree held up the bridesmaid dress that had been shredded.

"Goodness," the men gasped.

"I was sort of attacked and they tied me up with the

bridesmaid dress that Allegra stayed up all night making."

"Honey, they murdered that dress! We can't fix that," David said sympathetically.

"We happen to have this dress," Logan said, holding up the too-small one.

"But it's a good three sizes too small," Bree added.

"Come in, come in. When's the wedding and why can't Allegra work on it?" Josh asked as they followed him and David into a gorgeous, open condo.

"Allegra hasn't slept in forty-some hours because she had to remake the dress for me. She'd blow her lid if she saw this second dress destroyed. It's for Elle and Drake's wedding today."

Josh and David cringed. "Eww. We understand. We once saw her lose it behind the scenes of the Milan fashion show. And honey, it wasn't pretty."

David took the two dresses and draped them on a table. Both men looked over them for a while and talked.

Bree held her breath and prayed. After what seemed an eternity, they nodded and turned back to her. "We can fix it. Get undressed. We have some tummy sucker-uppers in the fitting room. Suck it all in, honey, and come on out," Josh ordered as he and David started gathering supplies.

Logan looked around helplessly. "I'll go get breakfast."

"Don't you dare!" Josh's eyes went wide at the horror of the idea. "She can't eat a thing or it'll never fit!"

"Coffee then, I'll go get coffee," Logan said, slightly scared of this whole situation.

"That would be lovely, thank you," David said with a smile.

"Oh, and if you don't want to see Bree naked and stuffed like a sausage, you may want to take at least forty-five minutes to get that coffee."

"Well, of course, I want to see her naked."

"Logan!" Bree shouted from the changing area.

"Oh," the men said knowingly. "So that's how it is then."

Logan sent them a full smile. "That's exactly how it is. I'll be back in ten."

Logan headed out the door with a smile still on his face as he heard the men gushing to Bree about her handsome beau.

"I'm stuck!" Bree cried from under miles of fabric. Her arms were above her head and David, Josh, and Logan were slowly working the gown over her head.

"Suck it in, honey," David told her as they gripped the fabric and continued to work it over her breasts and shoulders.

"Do I hear laughing?" Bree shot out. "Oh my gosh! Logan Ward, is that you?"

Logan smiled from his view as they peeled her out of the dress. "I'd never laugh at you, sweetheart. You know undressing you is my favorite activity."

"Swoon," Josh sighed as he and David laughed.

"I'm going to kill all of you when you get me out of this thing!"

"No, you're not. You're going to love and adore us," David said as they inched the dress up.

Bree let out an annoyed breath and the dress popped over her shoulders. The men pulled it over her head as her lungs expanded for the first time in the past hour.

"We can fix it. Now, I would advise not bending over or sitting down, but you'll be able to mostly breathe."

"Mostly?" Bree asked.

David sent her a wink and hurried to start taking the dress apart. Bree stood on the pedestal stuffed into the tightest corset the men had while Logan stood in front of her and just smiled at her breasts.

"Have I told you recently that I love you," Logan said with a boyish grin on his face.

Bree rolled her eyes and looked at the clock at the wall. "Oh shit!" She had twenty minutes to get to breakfast, and the only thing she had with her was the bloodstained outfit from last night.

"Take anything you want from the rack," Josh told her as he joined David. They fluidly worked as a pair, removing stitching and handing each other the tools they needed without saying a word.

"So, Logan, you're an architect? Have you ever designed a fashion boutique?"

"Can't say I have, though I would be up for it. I'm opening my own firm here in Atlanta."

Josh and David looked at each other and smiled. "Gee, I wonder why? When are you going to make an honest woman out of her?"

Logan didn't even mind the question. He'd thought about it since he discovered she wasn't married as he held her naked in his arms at the hospital. He'd known from that moment on this wasn't just a fling. It only took one taste of Bree to know she was the forever kind of woman. He'd had his one taste and now he wanted more.

"Soon. But it's our secret."

"We'll do your tuxedo. Our gift," Josh winked before they set back to work. Their hands flew over the material, and before Logan knew it, the dress was in pieces.

Bree ran out of the changing room in the most gorgeous

sundress he'd ever seen. The large white straps emphasized her bust, the tailored navy blue top made him want to put his hands on the curve of her waist where another white strip was calling to him.

He didn't have time to really look at the rest as she ran to Josh and David and gave them a kiss. "Meet me in the alley next to the church at five. Can you do that?"

"I have just the outfit for an incognito assignment," Josh teased. "Now shoo, let us work."

"You're the best!" Bree called out as she took Logan's hand and ran out the door.

Bree and Mallory looked nervously at the clock. Bree had five minutes until Josh and David were to arrive and everyone else was dressed and ready for pictures. Mallory, bless her heart, was doing everything she could to delay. She had just asked Bree for the third time to describe her heroics last night. Finally she got the text from Josh and David.

"Oh! It's Marcus, I'd better take this," Bree smiled and hurried from the room.

"Would you look at that?" Mallory said. "I left my dress in the car. You all get started on pictures. We'll just slip into our dresses and be right there."

Elle narrowed her eyes but didn't argue. Instead she ran a hand down her lace column dress and shook her head as the others left the room.

"Mallory, is this about my brother?" Elle asked once the room cleared.

"Reid? Why would you say that?" Mallory looked surprised as she had one foot out the door.

"It's just that you two seem odd. Come to think of it, I don't think I've seen you in the same room together since high school."

"Oh, please. He's your brother! You all are family," Mallory smiled and hoped Elle couldn't see her gritting her teeth.

"Phew, that makes me feel better," Elle smiled and held out her hands. "You are my third sister. You know that, right?"

"I do. You look breathtaking. Drake is one lucky man."

"I'm pretty lucky, too. Now, hurry and help Bree with whatever she's hiding and get your butt in the pictures."

Mallory raced from the dressing room out into the alley and froze. Bree was mostly naked in front of a van with one man holding her arms and another pulling hard on some strings.

"What on earth?"

"Corset," Bree said in a whoosh of air as the corset tightened. "Only way the dress will fit." She grunted as the man with the dark hair tied the strings.

"Well, hello! I'm Josh and that's David, and you should model for us."

Mallory just smiled and shook her head. Only Bree would go from steel-toed boots during the day surrounded by sweaty men, to a corset and a gown surrounded by two fashion designers who looked perfect enough to be cake toppers.

"Thanks, but no thanks. Don't worry, Bree. I have a knife to cut you out of that contraption."

Suddenly three pairs of eyes were on her. "Really? Where?" Josh asked as he gave the last tug on the corset.

"A lady never tells," Mallory grinned. "Well, since

you've got this, can I borrow the van to put my dress on?"

"Sure. We'll just be a moment more. Bree, no screaming this time," David lectured as he came at her with the dress.

Bree and Mallory hurried into the church where the ladies where having their pictures taken. Bree smiled and walked confidently in as she pretended she wasn't wearing a dress that was too small. The Bellerose men had done a number on it. While it was still too tight, they added some room to the bust and waist in the form of hidden panels or something like that. Bree didn't understand and she didn't care. Her boobs were perky, not mushed. And while she was corseted within an inch of her life, she could still take a breath. Sitting down was another matter.

"Sorry we're late! Marcus sends his love," Bree made up. She'd talked to Marcus on her way to the spa and was just now telling her family. He had cried when he heard the news that his mother was safe. He'd also tried to insist he needed to turn himself into the police. Instead, Bree had sent Agent Delmont over with Bree's personal attorney and made sure Marcus cleared his conscience, helped Delmont's case, and stayed out of jail. The result had been just that.

"Oh, send him our love," Margaret smiled. "I'll go see him tomorrow."

Allegra's eyes narrowed as she scanned Bree's dress. "Something isn't right."

Bree smiled and gave a little spin. "You worry too much. The dress is beautiful! Pictures?"

Soon the dress was the last thing on anyone's mind as Mary and Margaret helped fluff gowns and move people around as the photographer snapped pictures. Elle's excitement flowed all around the room. Bree was caught up in it as they made their way back into their dressing room to wait for the wedding. Bree fell behind the group and snuck out to find Logan sitting on a bench in the courtyard of the church.

"Wow. You look beautiful," Logan smiled as he stood up and gave her a soft lingering kiss on the lips.

"I only have a minute, but I just had to see you and make sure you were real."

"Real?"

"Logan, you're the best thing to ever happen to me. I saw how happy Elle is marrying Drake and it's the same happiness I feel when I'm with you. Thank you for everything—for loving me, for moving to Atlanta, for supporting me. Did I mention loving me?" Bree laughed lightly. Standing on her tiptoes she placed another kiss on his lips before hurrying back inside.

Logan watched his sunshine dart back inside the church and looked down at what he was working on in the shaded courtyard. It was coming together and soon he hoped he could present it as an engagement gift to his bride. There was no doubt he wanted to marry her. He loved all of her, from her mischievous plots to how she cared for each person she worked with. Life with Bree would never be dull, that's for sure. They would challenge each other to love more every day. Could there be anything better? Logan didn't think so as he got back to work on his surprise.

Mallory refused to look at the man walking her up the aisle. Reid Simpson had been dead to her for almost sixteen years. He was a stranger now . . . a stranger with large muscles that were straining to escape from under his tuxedo jacket, that is. They had smiled when Elle and Drake hurried up the aisle. And smiled as Bree and Phillip followed, both sending winks to their significant others. And they'd smiled as Allegra looped her arm through Drake's cousin's. They even smiled as Reid offered her his arm and Mallory took it. They just didn't smile at each other.

"Let's just get through this so we don't ruin my sister's day," Reid said as they walked up the aisle together.

"I would never do anything to hurt anyone in your family. I love them more than my own," Mallory shot back through her dazzling smile.

"We both know that's not true," Reid grunted before sending a wink to some bimbo in the crowd.

"Grow up, Reid. There's enough hurt and blame for everyone. It's time to move on."

"Say that if it makes you feel better, but after today I hope I never have to see you again."

Mallory felt the words like a million knives as they walked through the arched doors, and Reid dropped her hand, moving to congratulate his sister. So this was how it was going to be between them.

Chapter Twenty-Seven

"Bree!" Noah called as he ran into her office. "Big Al called and said you needed to get to the construction site immediately."

Bree shot from her chair. Today was the day they were going to be caught up. This was the day they were going to reach their first milestone. "What's wrong?"

"He didn't say. He just said you needed to hurry."

Bree grabbed a pair of socks from the drawer and put them on before she stuffed her feet into the steel-toed boots. She grabbed her pink hard hat from the corner of her desk and strode out of the office. Her black pencil skirt would be out of place on the job site, but the guys didn't care and she didn't want to take the time to change into jeans.

Everything had been going so perfectly since the night Jeff was arrested two weeks ago. The men were outraged and worked nonstop. She even picked up the rest of Jeff's workers as the government investigated the bribes and threats he doled out in order to get contracts. Work at the site was a hive of activity.

And every night she went home to Logan. It was perfect. She ended and began each day with a kiss from Logan. At night he'd tell her about all the places he'd visited in his quest for the perfect office building for his new firm. Just yesterday, he'd told her he'd found one downtown that he was thinking about buying. They'd sat together under the stars and talked. They'd walked through the historic parts of the city. And every night, when they fell into bed, there was no question of them being made for each other. So, why did something have to go wrong today? Today, when she'd been planning a surprise romantic weekend at the family getaway spot.

As she pulled up to the work site, she saw the problem immediately. No one was there. How could they get the work done when no one was there? Bree hurried from her car and stopped at the gate. A large piece of paper with some drawn plans was nailed to it. It looked to be redesigned plans of her building, but it focused on the top floor. Looking up, she saw that no windows had been installed and just the skeleton of the upper floors was finished. The mesh protective covering prevented her from seeing if anything had happened to the area. What worried her upon further examination of the new drawing was that something had been drawn in the middle of the floor. Oh no! She hoped the guys didn't build the hideous statue Marcus had requested in order to delay the build.

Bree hurried into the building and took the service elevator up to the top. She pulled the doors open and stepped out into the large open floor with confusion. All her workers were gathered in a circle with worried looks on their faces.

"Miss Simpson," Big Al called as he hurried forward. "We don't know what to do; the plans have been changed again."

"I saw them on the fence. What on earth?" Bree asked as the men started moving out of her way.

Logan was in the center of the circle down on one knee. As she gasped, the men's worried faces turned to huge smiles. Bree felt her hands start to shake as she stepped into the middle of the circle of workers. She felt Big Al standing behind her and could hear some sniffles coming from his direction.

"Bree Simpson, you are the most remarkable woman I've ever had the good fortune to meet. Of course, it started out rough, but just look at what we turned it into." Bree chuckled along with her whole crew. "I didn't realize I had stopped living my life until I met you. But now I want more, and you've given me the desire to break free of the past. All I see is a bright future as long as you're by my side. This building brought us together, so I thought this would be the perfect place for me to ask you this. Bree, will you marry me?"

Bree looked down at the ring Logan produced from his pocket. The roomful of people was quiet except for some sniffles and a sob from Big Al. Bree saw a flash of color to her side and the men stepping aside for Allegra and her mother. Their eyes shone with unshed tears as they smiled. But when she looked at Logan, it was as if they all disappeared. He was her heart, her love, her husband.

"Yes! Yes, I'll marry you," Bree grinned as she held out a shaky hand for him to put the ring on. The crew erupted in cheers as Logan swooped her up into his arms and kissed her.

"You're my world and I'll love you until my dying breath and beyond," Logan whispered into her ear before kissing tears of joy from her cheek.

"I love you, too, Logan . . . so very much."

"Oh, come over here, you two!" Margaret cried as she hurried forward with her arms open and Allegra close behind. Carolyn Ward smiled shyly from behind Bree's family.

"You invited your mother!"

"I did. I think she was inspired by your confidence and has finally stood up for herself. She marched my father and brother over to the house yesterday and demanded they apologize to me. I wouldn't be surprised if she grabs them by the ear and drags them into your office as well."

"I'm glad you're rebuilding a relationship with your family. Family is so important to me, so the effort means a lot."

"I think after I realized I didn't need their approval, it became a lot easier to work on forgiving them for their mistakes and moving on. I could waste my life being mad at my dad for not showing his love, or at Stacy and Brad for their betrayal, but I'd rather spend my time loving you."

"Oh, we're so happy," Margaret said excitedly when she reached them. Bree laughed as she and Logan were pulled into a tight hug. "Carolyn and I are already planning the engagement shower."

"Mom," Bree and Logan both whined. They laughed at each other and Bree decided now might not be the time to tell her mom she dreamed of marrying Logan in a quiet ceremony at their family retreat and not in some large wedding. She'd ruin her mother's dream later.

The sound of a horn startled the group. When Bree turned to see what it was, she found Big Al with a handkerchief and a smile. He came forward, and the crowd hushed.

"We all have an engagement gift for the best boss there is." Al handed her a piece of paper. Bree opened it and saw the stamp from the inspector. They had officially reached their second milestone ahead of time. The bonus would be enough to pay all the additional workers.

"Thank you all for your hard work. We couldn't have

reached this milestone without it. I appreciate every minute you put into this building. Now let's celebrate!" The men cheered, and Noah pressed the music button on the boombox. The floor was filled with well wishes, laughter, and some karaoke of "We Built This City."

Logan couldn't stop smiling as he drove Bree to his surprise. The party with the construction crew and her family had been perfect for them. They had sung karaoke quite badly, laughed, and danced on top of the partially constructed building, the building that had brought them together.

"Aren't we close to David and Josh's place?"

"Yes we are. This is the new warehouse district. These old warehouses have been transformed into luxury condos. There's a large park just behind us and lots of mom-and-pop restaurants are opening along here as well," Logan told her as he pulled up to a building with a For Sale sign in the window.

"I just love this part of town. It's so quaint. And for some reason I feel right at home with all the brick and steel," Bree joked.

"That's why I brought you here." Logan reached behind Bree and handed her a large tube.

"What's this?" she asked as she opened it and pulled out the large sheet of paper.

"It's a gift for both of us."

Logan held his breath as Bree unrolled the paper and looked at it. After a moment, her head shot up as she looked at the building in front of them and then back down at the paper.

"Are these plans for turning this warehouse into a home?"

"A house and an office for Ward Architecture. That bottom corner could be my office and there would be space right next door for an office for you when you work from home."

"This is amazing. I love it, Logan. Can we see inside?"

"Of course. I called the Realtor; he's here to let us in."

Logan watched with excitement as Bree refused to put down the plans. They walked to the door that would serve as his office. A man opened it for them with a smile and then headed outside to wait as Bree looked around with an eye honed from a job in construction.

"Look at this exposed brick. It's beautiful. The mortar is in good shape and we could really emphasize those beams up there. This will be a beautiful office, Logan." Bree hurried from the room and opened another door. "Would this be my office?"

"Yes. And I can put in a door there to lead directly into the house."

Bree squealed and hurried from the room with her face buried in his plans. She opened the door leading to the main part of the warehouse that would serve as their home. Logan followed her with pride and a new certainty. This was his life. Making Bree smile was all he wanted. But the feeling he got drawing up plans to make other people this happy made him know starting his own firm was the right thing to do.

"Oh wow," Bree gasped as they entered what would be the open living room, dining room, and kitchen.

Logan came up behind her and wrapped his arms around her. "Can't you see it—our life here? I see you working at your desk overlooking the park. I see family dinners, kids running around as I chase them, a pair of muddy boots, and a hook for a pink hard hat right there by the door."

Bree turned in his arms and cupped his face with her hands. "I can see it, and I can't wait to start our lives together." Bree kissed him lightly on the lips, and Logan felt all the love and promise of a future in it. "Let's buy it."

"I'll get the agent."

"Logan," Bree stopped him from leaving. "I don't want to wait to start living our lives together. How does eloping sound?"

"I think your mother would kill us."

"I was always the troublemaker. It shouldn't surprise her. How does next week sound?"

"I think it sounds like seven days too long."

"Our family has a private island off the coast of Connecticut," Bree said. "It's ten acres and there's a main house, but there's also a romantic cabin on the other side of the island overlooking the ocean."

"As long as I get to marry you, I don't care where I am."

"We'd better break the news to our mothers," Bree said as she cringed.

"We'll just tell them it gives us a head start on working on grandchildren, and I think they'll forgive us." Logan winked.

"I don't think I've been so excited to find out what the future holds as I am now. I love you, Logan Ward."

Epilogue

One week later . . .

The weather was perfect. A gentle breeze washed in from the ocean and sent the bride's fingertip veil fluttering. Allegra clasped the bouquet of wildflowers in her hand as she watched her sister say "I do" to a beaming Logan. Their smiles were brighter than the setting sun behind them.

Allegra had locked herself up with Josh and David to complete the wedding dress and tuxedo in time. But it was worth it to see her sister so happy. The tea-length chiffon dress looked whimsical with its ruched bodice and flowing skirt. It was perfect for this casual wedding. They were on the well-manicured lawn of the estate, lined on one side by thick trees and on the other by the ocean.

Looking out at the small crowd, Allegra smiled at where her family sat with Shirley. Only Mallory was missing. She had a job out of the country, or so she had said. Noah, Finn, Josh, and David took up the next row. Even the Wards had flown in for the celebration. Bree hadn't told her much, but she could tell there was tension there. It appeared, as Logan's mother dabbed her eyes, that they were working on it. After all, family was hard work.

"I now pronounce you husband and wife; you may kiss

your bride."

Allegra felt a tear run down her cheek as Logan dipped Bree and kissed her to the resounding cheers of the family and guests. Her eyes automatically traveled to Finn. She blushed when she realized he was looking right at her as he clapped. The happy couple hurried down the grassy aisle, and Allegra linked arms with Logan's best friend from London.

Pictures had been taken, toasts had been given, and the first dance had just begun. Allegra felt her phone buzz in her clutch as she watched Logan worship her sister on the small dance floor by the main house. Fighting the urge to look at her email, she pulled it up anyway. With Fashion Week just a month away, she needed to make sure it wasn't an emergency.

My Dearest Love,

I don't understand why you insist on hurting me. We were meant for each other. You need to stop denying it and come back to me. You owe me. If I can't have you, I don't see the reason for us to live anymore. I certainly won't sit back and watch you act the whore for some chauffeur. I see the way you look at him and I won't allow it. There has always been and will always be only me for you.

Allegra started to shake. He wouldn't leave her alone. She knew their break-up had been hard. But the messages he continued to send her over the past year were getting progressively more threatening.

"You look stunning tonight, Allegra." The voice made her jump and she shoved the phone into her bra as if it were something bad she had to hide. "Are you okay? Whoa, something is the matter. What is it?"

"Finn," Allegra said as she put a hand over her wild heart. "Nothing, I'm fine. You just surprised me. I was just thinking how wonderful it is that my two sisters are so happy."

Finn stood close to her in his steel-gray suit as she battled with her thoughts. Would he hurt Finn? She had been trying to hide her feelings for just that reason. Behind her cheerful smile, there was a storm she didn't want to drag anyone into.

She didn't jump this time when she felt Finn's hand slide down her arm and take her hand in his. It felt safe. It felt adventurous. It felt kind. The simple touch was enough to start her heart dancing. When she looked up into his eyes, she saw the interest she felt returned. She saw he wanted the same thing she did — more.

"Will you dance with me?"

Allegra nodded and let Finn lead her onto the dance floor. He pulled her in close. She smelled the gentle scent of cedar as his hand gently slid down her back. Beneath his suit, his muscles tightened in response to her. Finn bent his head next to hers. She felt his hot breath on her neck as he slowly led her around the floor. Surely they were safe on the private island, and she could give into her feelings. She felt her phone vibrate again and knew the cold hard truth. She had to protect Finn. And to do so meant she could never be with him. She could never be with anyone ever again.

Made in the USA
Lexington, KY
27 May 2015